IN THE HOURS SINCE THE BOYS HAD DISCOVERED HIM, DANIEL HAD SLOWLY, ERRATICALLY, COME BACK TO LIFE.

His body temperature was on the rise, and his cells were beginning to thaw. He knew he was alive – every muscle, sinew and organ in his body was aflame with pain – but that was all he knew ...

He found Nat's jacket and, with immense effort, managed to tie the garment around his waist. Then he began to walk, stumbling through the maze of crates and barrels, moving only inches at a time. His eyes were fast recovering, adjusting to the gloom ... He was terrified.

Through a foggy haze, a jumble of memories, a single clear thought emerged: *Harry! He had to find Harry!*

ROBERT TINE

FOREVER YOUNG

Based on the screenplay by
Jeffrey Abrams

A SIGNET BOOK

SIGNET

Published by the Penguin Group
Penguin Books Ltd, 27 Wrights Lane, London w8 5tz, England
Penguin Books USA Inc., 375 Hudson Street, New York, New York 10014, USA
Penguin Books Australia Ltd, Ringwood, Victoria, Australia
Penguin Books Canada Ltd, 10 Alcorn Avenue, Toronto, Ontario, Canada m4v 3b2
Penguin Books (NZ) Ltd, 182–190 Wairau Road, Auckland 10, New Zealand

Penguin Books Ltd, Registered Offices: Harmondsworth, Middlesex, England

First published in the USA 1992
First published in Great Britain 1993
1 3 5 7 9 10 8 6 4 2

Signet Film and TV Tie-in edition first published 1992

Typeset by Datix International Limited, Bungay, Suffolk
Printed in England by Clays Ltd, St Ives plc

PART ONE

CHAPTER ONE

You could sense it before you could hear it, hear it before you could see it.

The air in the clear, still blue sky suddenly started to quiver as if turning restless, pulsing uneasily. It was as if a storm was just over the horizon, winds and thunder were about to burst. Then came the deep drone, far off, the purr of powerful engines and the shimmering blades of heavy propellers thrashing the air. The sound grew in intensity. The hum became a wail, then a roar, as all 111 feet of the turbocharged B-25, both engines pounding, blasted through the sky.

The sleek fighter bomber was silver and as graceful as a shark, and from the ground it looked like an aluminum bullet streaking through the air. The plane flew without markings or numbers; no external sign betrayed the make or type of aircraft. This twin-engined medium bomber was still a secret prototype, a hush-hush weapon being developed by the United States Army Air Corps.

From outside, the plane looked serene, all-powerful, but the view from within was considerably less calm. The cockpit was a nest of wires and gauges, a tangle of cable hastily taped to the support structure of the tiny cabin. The B-25 was still very much a work in progress, and the compartment had been hastily jerry-rigged, a snarled and twisted pocket of improvised wiring and electronics. Only when the big problems with the prototype were worked out would the engineers turn to the task of prettifying the interior.

In the meantime the thrown-together cabin would have to do. Lieutenant Daniel McCormick sat in the middle of all the disorder, his hands locked tight on the control yoke. The mass and clutter were not the problem pressing most on the mind of the pilot.

The prototype had been rushed into the air well before it was ready. It was apparent that the nation – the whole world – was rushing headlong toward war, and the Army Air Corps was determined to have this craft in production before the storm of hostility broke.

From behind the dark lenses of his aviator glasses McCormick scanned the rows of dials and gauges in front of him, reading the information and transmitting it back to his base command center. The airfield was 20,000 feet below and 5 miles away to the west.

The nose of the plane was down, and the needle of the altimeter was dropping quickly.

"We're coming through angels nineteen," he yelled into the microphone. The noise of the engines was deafening in the not yet soundproofed cockpit. "Angels nineteen" was pilot slang for 19,000 feet – and falling.

Instantly a voice crackled in his headset, a voice that sounded strained and anxious. "Viper one, take it easy!"

Daniel hardly heard it. The plane had lost another 500 feet of altitude, and he could feel that there wasn't enough power left in the engines to pull the aircraft out of its dangerous dive.

"I'm throttling back," Daniel shouted. "I'm at eighteen five. Revs at thirty-two hundred."

"Watch your pressure," cautioned control.

Daniel slapped the oil-pressure meter set in the dashboard. "Can't watch the pressure. Needle's stuck.

We're in the green." The plane was beginning a sickening spiral toward the dun-colored earth. "I'm at seventeen five."

The howl of the engines turned rough and uneven. The aircraft juddered, and the thrashing of the motors threatened to beat the frail fuselage to pieces. In a matter of seconds the craft lost another 2,000 feet. "Fifteen five! Clear skies! VSI over two thousand! We've got negative buffet!" He took a deep breath and wiped the sweat from his forehead. "Oh, brother . . ."

It was a test pilot's job to try to wreck his aircraft, to push a plane beyond its specifications, to put the aircraft and pilot in harm's way intentionally just to see what would happen. But the ground seemed alarmingly close – and was rapidly getting closer.

The plane shuddered and bucked like a stallion trying to unseat his rider. It had become several tons of uncertain metal reeling in the sky.

"Woah! She's purring all right!" Daniel shouted as the machine rocked and flapped in the clear blue sky.

"Bring her back, Viper One. Bring her back to base."

Daniel could hardly hear ground control over the noise of the screaming metal and the clamor of the engines.

Daniel thought this was a great idea. "Roger! She's buckling! I'm pulling out! I'm gonna bring it back!" *I think*, he added mentally.

"Increase your back pressure."

Daniel fell on the throttles and pulled back hard. "Increasing!" The plane jumped again and the body rumbled like thunder. "I've got serious buckling. It's hard to keep her on the straight and narrow." He grappled with the steering mechanism. "The controls are resisting."

It took all his strength to get the plane on course for the airfield as he wrestled it through the sky. It took him a full five minutes of tussling to pull the aircraft on to the route to safety.

McCormick tore his eyes from the control panel long enough for a quick glimpse out of the starboard window of the cockpit. He could make out the airfield a few miles off to his right, a dark smudge of tarmac runways against the dry, pale-brown scrub.

"Home, please, James," he muttered to himself.

Three miles away a group of men stood on the airfield hardstand worriedly scanning the skies. The airstrip was a dilapidated, run-down collection of hangars and sheds, an agglomeration of buildings that hardly merited the grand name the Army Air Corps had hung on them: the Douglas Military Research Facility.

A dozen engineers and technicians were huddled around a metal table set up on the tarmac. The surface of the table was strewn with blueprints and manuals, acres of close-printed paper offering a million technical details on the airplane that was battling its way back to the airport. There was a big vacuum-tube radio set up there too, the speaker alive with the crackle of static and Daniel's frantic stream of situation reports from the rattling cockpit of the B-25.

No one paid any attention as a car, a Hudson Terraplane, roared across the field and screeched to a halt next to the crowd of worried technicians. Harry Finley, Daniel's best friend and research scientist at the base, tumbled out of the car, his arms full of charts and manuals as well as a giant red-leather-bound notebook. He added the charts and manuals to the riot of papers already lying on the table but kept the red notebook tucked protectively under his arms.

"Where's Daniel?"

A technician pointed to the sky. "He's still up there."

The radio burst into life. "Fourteen thousand feet!" Daniel announced. "Negative buffet! Repeat: negative buffet!"

"Sure hope I made those bolts *real tight*," muttered one of the engineers.

All eyes were on the sky now, scanning the blue canopy for a sign of the B-25.

"There he is!"

One of the technicians was pointing straight off toward the horizon. The B-25 was slipping in toward the field, and the watchers on the ground could see that Daniel had begun all the classic maneuvers for a crash landing. He had opened the fuel tanks, and the excess gasoline was pouring from the wing vats like a cloudburst. The engines and the electrical systems had been shut down – the pilot didn't want a single piece of hot metal or the tiniest spark in the air to touch off a fire. The flaps were dropped down as low as they would go, slowing the flight speed; the giant aircraft was now nothing more than a huge kite slowly sinking toward the ground.

The B-25 hit the ground like a belly-flopping diver, the underside of the machine slapping on to the runway. The force of impact threw the plane back into the air a few feet, then slammed it down again. The port wing dipped, and the wing-tip stuck in the ground. With a shriek of tortured metal the wing pulled free from the fuselage.

Pieces of rubble flew through the air like spray as the rest of the machine plowed across the field. The tail came down hard, and the rear stabilizers snapped off as if they were built of nothing more substantial than balsa wood.

The plane plunged forward like a torpedo, kicking up a 20-foot wall of earth and turf, digging a trench for 300 yards. Then it came to a halt, the B-25's nose buried in the earth, the wrecked aircraft wreathed in a huge cloud of smoke and dust. For a moment the silence was dreadful.

The men assembled on the field were off and running toward the wreck. Emergency vehicles, fire trucks, ambulances, raced across the field. No one, not even Harry, could believe that the pilot had survived such a hideous crash.

Then the escape hatch opened above the cockpit, and Daniel hauled himself out. His face was filthy and running with sweat; his clothes were torn and dirty; his hair was in wild disarray. But his smile was brilliant. "If she comes with a warranty," he shouted gleefully, "I'll take her!"

CHAPTER TWO

The rescue crews and the technicians burst into laughter, and there was a smattering of applause as Daniel climbed down from the smoking wreck of the B-25. Harry, relieved, allowed himself to take the first breath he had drawn in some minutes.

Technicians were swarming over the plane, and a doctor was bearing down on Daniel like a gundog after a bird that had just been shot out of the sky.

"I hope you're not married to those Pratt and Whitney engines," Daniel announced to the engineers. "A classic plane needs classic engines." He turned to his friend. "Harry!" He seemed elated, still high on the adrenalin rush of the crash. "Did you see that? Was that some doozy of a crash or what?"

"What, Danny? Did I see what?" Harry asked nonchalantly.

A photographer rushed over and raised his giant Speed Graphic camera like a double-barrel shotgun. "How's about a picture for *Stars and Stripes*, lieutenant?"

Harry turned and, striking a mock-heroic pose, grinned for the signalman. "Make sure you get my good side."

Flash bulbs popped, blinding Daniel for a moment. The doctor appeared at his elbow, just as he snuck a Lucky Strike cigarette from the pack in his breast pocket.

"Lieutenant," asked the doctor, frowning down at a

clipboard and at the cigarette, "did you experience any dizziness? Or fainting?"

Daniel blew out a great blue cloud of cigarette smoke. "No."

"Did you feel lightheaded?"

"Nope. Harry, do *you* feel lightheaded?"

Harry was leaning against his jeep, wiping his brow with a snowy white handkerchief. "No. I'm still having a heart attack."

Daniel grinned. "Yeah! Looked pretty darned good, didn't it?"

"Oh, yeah, Danny. That landing was a work of art."

"Was there queasiness?" asked one of the doctors.

"No. Harry, I thought you weren't coming out of that hole of yours until you finished your experiment."

"Blackout? Did you black out?" asked the doctor.

"No."

Harry stowed his handkerchief in his back pocket. "Just promise me . . . Promise me you'll never work for an airline."

Daniel laughed heartily. "Tell me honestly, Harry. Right at the end – you were worried, weren't you? Betcha thought I wasn't going to pull up, did you?"

"Well, it crossed my mind."

"Was there blindness?"

"No."

"Headache?"

"No."

"How about chest pain?"

"No." Harry had fallen in alongside Daniel, and the two men, trailed by the doctor, walked toward Harry's car. "Harry, I was *so* close to the ground I could have read your license plate – and all of a sudden, I see Helen."

Now it was the doctor's turn to be startled. "You had a *vision*? Did you vomit?"

Daniel stopped and grabbed the doctor by the collar. "No. There was no vomit. Listen, doc, I'm trying to talk to my friend here. We'll do the big question-and-answer session a little later. Okay?"

The doctor smiled weakly. "Gee, sure thing, lieutenant. Nice landing. See you later."

Daniel turned back to Harry. "I thought of Helen. I thought: *she's coming back tonight. I better pull up.* Then *wham*! I hit the ground."

"Just like that?"

Daniel nodded. "Just like that."

The crash was already a fast receding memory. "Hey – what are you doing for dinner? I was thinking ribs. What do you think? Ribs?"

Eating was the furthest thing from Harry's mind right at that moment. *"Danny . . ."* He took a deep breath. "I came out to the field because . . . because it worked."

"Worked? What worked?"

"What do you think? My experiment. It's still a little rough around the edges . . . but it definitely worked."

It took a moment for the import of Harry's words to sink in. A shocked, slightly puzzled smile crossed Danny's face as he assembled all the facts in his mind.

"What? You mean . . . it *worked*?"

Harry laughed giddily. "Yes, that's right. I froze Buford."

For a moment both men were lightheaded, like two kids sharing an incredible, implausible secret.

Harry did his best to act serious. "No I

can know about this."

Daniel wasn't quite ready to calm d

incredible! Harry, you're a genius." Abru

his friend square in the eye. "No one can

"That's right."

"It's got to be our secret."

"Absolutely!"

"*Helen* can know."

Harry was reluctant. "Helen can kno

Helen, all right? Because it *is* incredible

groped for words and came up empty.

well, incredible." He threw up his hands.

"It is," agreed Daniel. "I'll clean

celebrate, okay?" He slapped Harry he

back and started running toward the ba

ping off his parachute harness as he went.

"Yeah, okay," Harry yelled after him.

ing."

"I'm driving," insisted Daniel.

"Forget it. I'm driving!"

"*I*'m driving."

"There's no *way* he's driving," Harry

CHAPTER THREE

Being a test pilot for the Army Air Corps was an exciting career if not a particularly well-paying one. Daniel McCormick could barely pay the rent on his small apartment, so there was not all that much money left over to pay for furniture. There wasn't much in the living room except for a Howard cabinet radio, a battered couch and a single comfortable armchair. The radio played softly, but Daniel, undisturbed by the silky tones of Billie Holiday's "The Very Thought of You," was slumped low in the chair, sound asleep.

The room looked as if it had been the site of a party held at the same time as some kind of scientific seminar. There were empty bottles and half-full glasses standing on the floor in the midst of a riot of aviation plans and technical texts. Full ashtrays were strewn about among scientific instruments.

Daniel snored slightly, his mouth open. There was a pile of papers and notes resting on his chest, topped by a glass ashtray that rose and fell and wobbled precariously as he breathed.

Helen stood in the doorway of the room, a camera slung over one shoulder, a light suitcase in her right hand. She looked at Daniel and smiled to herself, then put down her luggage. Helen had dark hair and fair skin and big dark-brown eyes that glittered in the few rays of light that penetrated the room.

She leaned down and kissed him, her lips brushing lightly across his. It was a tender touch that barely nudged Daniel toward wakefulness. His eyes remained closed, but he definitely responded, kissing her warm lips. Then, almost as if it was happening in slow motion, Daniel grew more passionate, the kiss rising to a peak, then falling back to become softer, gentler. Helen pulled back.

Eyes still closed, Daniel spoke. "Wait a minute. Who *is* that?"

Helen laughed and nudged him, and he pulled her into his lap and hugged her close.

"I'm sorry I'm so late." She spoke in a quiet, hushed tone as if trying to avoid disturbing the silence of the night.

"What time is it?"

"Almost two."

"Why so late?"

"There was a problem on the train tracks or something or other. I was going to go to my place, but I wanted to see you. Hope you don't mind."

"I sort of do," he said with a small smile. "Would you leave, please?"

She leaned forward to kiss him again. "Sure."

"So how did it go?"

Helen shook her head as if trying to forget what she had seen. Her assignment had been back east, photographing the victims of the Dust Bowl and the strikers at the steel mills. "It was depressing. These people have nothing. Nothing at all." She brushed a tangle of hair from his eyes. "You need a haircut."

"Yeah, I know. Barber shop was closed all weekend." She was leaning forward, a small gold locket hanging on a fine gold chain dangling in his eyes. "I gave you this so you'd put a picture of me in it."

"I will . . . as soon as you let me take one of you."
She kissed him lightly. "Mmmmmmmm . . . you taste
like champagne."

"Harry and I got a little drunk," said Daniel a touch
sheepishly.

Helen pulled back and looked into his blue eyes.
"Oh, yeah? A celebration?"

"Sort of. You must be hungry."

"I am."

Daniel pushed her aside and stood up. "Then I think it
is time for one of my famous omelets." He led the way
into the small kitchen. He busied himself with a cast-iron
skillet, which he greased with butter. Then he started
breaking eggs into a bowl, beating them vigorously.

"Let me see the work. The pictures."

"Later,' said Helen.

"No," Daniel insisted, "now."

"They're not really the kind of thing you look at
over dinner."

"I have a strong stomach."

"But I'm the one eating."

"Well, you have a stronger stomach than I do."

The pictures were just as powerful as she said they
were, black-and-white photos of the sad, the broken,
the dirt-poor of the great Depression.

Daniel slid the omelet out of the frying pan and on to
her plate, folding the eggs perfectly. He picked up one of
the pictures and stared at it intently. It was a photograph
of a worker standing outside the gates of the steel mill
where he had worked until being locked out by the
owners. He was stoop-shouldered and as thin as a knife
blade. In his gnarled arms he held a dirty-faced infant
who stared, uncomprehendingly, into the camera lens.

The picture captured all the conflicting emotions of the hopeless man. Anger, fear and desperation seemed to radiate from his slumped shoulders, imprinting themselves on the photographic plate.

"Wow," said Daniel. "That is powerful."

Helen frowned. "I don't know. I'm not sure it's right."

"Right? It's a masterpiece. Any fool can see that. Definitely," Daniel insisted.

She put the picture aside. "Any fool?" she said with a laugh.

"Eat."

Helen picked up the fork and began to eat heartily. "So what were you celebrating? Let me guess. Harry's four-hundredth consecutive hour in the laboratory?"

"Close. How's the omelet?"

"Danny, I've been eating *dust* for three days."

"That good, huh?"

"That good. So what were you celebrating? The real question being, of course, why wasn't I invited?"

"Well . . ." Daniel wondered exactly how she was going to take this. "Harry froze a chicken."

Helen almost laughed out loud. "Oh, wow! My *butcher*'s done that."

"Yeah, but your butcher never brought his chicken back to life, has he?"

Helen stopped eating, the fork halfway between the plate and her mouth. "What?"

"Your butcher has never done that – unless he has, in which case he and Harry oughta have a talk. Because, you have to admit, that *is* quite a coincidence."

"Harry did *what*?"

"I know, I know, it's impossible. At least, it was

impossible until today. Harry is a genius. Which he himself was insisting after the second bottle, if you can imagine. It was pretty ugly."

"I can imagine."

"'Now,' said Daniel soberly, "this part is real important. No one can know about this."

Helen smiled wrily. "What? It's a big government frozen-chicken conspiracy? One of those?"

"You can't tell anyone. I promised Harry you wouldn't tell anyone. Now you promise me . . ."

"Okay. No one but my mother."

"Helen!"

"I'm kidding," she insisted. "Joke."

"Promise?"

Helen nodded. "I promise."

"Even under torture?" asked Daniel.

"Even under torture."

A mischievous gleam suddenly lit up in Daniel's eyes. "Even under T torture?"

"Danny." She shivered. "T" torture was her greatest fear – and Daniel knew it.

Daniel began to move toward her, low to the ground like a cat advancing on an unsuspecting pigeon.

"Danny, don't." She was already starting to giggle a little in anticipation of what was coming.

Daniel moved in closer, until he was looming over her. "Don't what?"

"Don't tickle me!" she shouted, overcome with laughter. "You tickle me, and I'm going to scream! Danny!"

His hands were out in front of him, his fingers wiggling like tentacles. "Helen, this is a matter of national security. I have to be sure I can trust you."

Then he attacked, his fingers dancing wildly over her ribs, tickling her mercilessly.

"DANNY! NO!" She was choking with laughter, doubling over against his onslaught, trying to protect herself from his prying hands and fingers. "I won't tell!" She wriggled and screamed under the exquisite torture. "Never! I won't!"

As suddenly as he started he stopped, his torment replaced by kisses.

"I missed you," he said.

CHAPTER FOUR

Twice every summer the entire team working on the development of the B-25 at the Douglas Military Research Facility took the day off and had a picnic. Everyone, from the project director down to the mechanic crews, attended, egghead engineers mixing with burly ground-crew airmen. There was even a baseball game between the aeronautical engineers and the enlisted men. Inevitably, the enlisted men always beat the tar out of the intellectuals.

The picnics drew whole families – the events were particular favorites with kids and dogs – who came bearing full picnic baskets ready to share their fried chicken and potato salad with all comers.

There were little knots of people all over the field: fathers and sons playing catch, barbecuers coughing and gagging over their smoky fires. A teenager threw a stick for a big, shaggy dog.

In a far corner of the field an aircrew sergeant had taken it upon himself to teach the basics of baseball to the son of one of the engineers. It was hard work.

"See," he explained patiently, "if the man on second base touches the man who's running with the ball, then the runner is out."

"But why is the man running in the first place?"

The sergeant sighed. "Okay, we're gonna start over . . ."

Daniel and Helen sat on a blanket with Harry, his wife Blanche and a few of the research crew. A few yards away a child, half of a vanilla ice-cream cone spread across his fat cheeks, stood watching every move Daniel made. The kid was fascinated by him, watching in awe as he ate a sandwich and consumed a bottle of orange Nehi as if the child had never seen a creature so strange or behavior so bizarre.

The scrutiny was beginning to bother Daniel. "This kid," he muttered to Helen, "he keeps staring at me."

Helen glanced at the boy and flashed him a big smile. "He likes you."

"Likes me? He doesn't even know me."

Surprisingly, none of the talk at the picnic centered on the development of the B-25. The problems of the aircraft occupied their every waking hour during the week, and no one wanted to think about them on a rare, precious day off.

The big story of the week was the retirement from baseball of the great New York Yankees first baseman, the Iron Horse of baseball, Lou Gehrig. He had stood at home plate in Yankee Stadium and had announced to the shocked crowd that he had contracted a degenerative muscular disease, amyothropic lateral sclerosis. No one could pronounce it, so the fatal illness had been quickly dubbed "Lou Gehrig's disease". In spite of this he had proclaimed himself happy and satisfied with his lot.

"He said he was the luckiest man on the face of the earth," said Daniel. "Brother, there is *never* going to be another Lou Gehrig."

"Could we talk about something less depressing?" said Helen. "Pass the coleslaw."

"Well, we have news," said Harry. "A little announcement." He cleared his throat portentously.

"Yeah?" said Daniel.

"Next year," he glanced at his wife, "next year Blanche will be celebrating her first Mother's Day!"

"And you're going to be celebrating Father's Day for the first time," said Blanche, happily.

"You dog!" exclaimed Daniel.

"Gee," said Helen with a smile. "How did that happen, Harry? Did Blanche have to go to the laboratory? Where did you two ever find the time?"

"Oh, stop it," said Blanche, her cheeks reddening.

"We just found out," said Harry sheepishly.

Daniel raised his soda. "To Harry junior!"

"To Harriet!" said Helen.

She was smiling, delighted at the good fortune of her friends, but behind her smile there was a little touch of sorrow and envy. Daniel caught the sad expression on her face, but immediately looked away, unwilling to meet her unspoken question.

CHAPTER FIVE

Jake's Diner on Main Street in down-town Douglas, California, was a regular stop for Daniel. He looked in almost every day for a cup of coffee or a piece of pie or a burger – he liked the place. It was unpretentious. The food was good. The waiters and waitresses knew him. He felt at home there.

He was so much at home and the employees knew him so well that they paid no attention whatsoever when Helen got up to use the phone in the booth in the corner of the restaurant. Daniel began talking earnestly and with great sincerity. Alone.

The words did not come easily to him. He drew a deep breath and launched into his speech, his eyes darting nervously toward the phone booth, afraid that Helen would come back and catch him.

"Look. We're . . . we, uh . . ." He stopped like a car running out of gasoline. He thought for a moment, then started again. "It's 1939 already. And . . . well, like you said, we're not kids anymore. Not getting any younger."

Daniel cleared his throat nervously. "Look, you usually get my thoughts before I do, so . . . you probably know what I'm gonna say. Helen, will you marry me?"

He sat back in the booth. "There. I said it."

The waiter delivered a cup of coffee to his table. "It was a very pretty speech, Danny. You should try it when Helen is here. You might even get an answer. That would be really interesting, don't you think?"

"That's the next step," said Daniel. "She'll be off the phone in a minute. In the meantime I have to rehearse."

He took another deep breath. "Helen, you know, I've been thinking . . ."

"Danny!" Helen was bustling across the restaurant, a huge grin on her face. She threw herself into the seat across from Daniel.

"Guess what. *Collier's Magazine* wants my pictures for their November issue."

"Hey, really? That's great news."

"They say it's kind of a rush thing," she said quickly, reaching for his hand. "They say they need the prints by the – ooops!"

She had knocked over a salt shaker. Helen was not superstitious, but she wasn't taking any chances either. She poured a few grains of salt into the palm of her hand and tossed them over her left shoulder.

"They say they need the prints by Thursday, which means they have to be ready by tomorrow afternoon, which means I gotta get to work . . . Which means I gotta go . . ."

Daniel panicked. "*Wait.* Uh, want some pie?"

Helen looked at her boyfriend as if he had just in that moment lost his mind.

"But, Danny, we just *had* pie."

Daniel thought fast. "Oh, sure, we had *cherry* pie. We didn't have the *blueberry* pie. Did we? Admit it."

"No, we didn't."

"See?"

She shook her head in disbelief. "How can you still be hungry?"

Daniel shrugged. "Heck, I don't know. Isn't that

23

the darnedest thing?" He flagged down the waiter. "Can we get some blueberry pie over here? Sure you don't want a piece? It's really good."

Daniel McCormick was, perhaps, the most inept liar in the entire state of California, and Helen was as sharp as a tack. She peered at him quizzically.

"Danny, what's going on?"

Daniel avoided looking at her questioning gaze, his eyes darting around the room, looking at anything and anybody rather than her. "What's going on? Nothing's going on. I just want you to sit with me while I finish my lunch."

"Danny, I *have* to get going."

"I'll eat fast."

But Helen was still suspicious. "Wait, you're not trying to break some news to me, are you? Something you know I don't want to hear?"

"No, no. Really." Actually, he wasn't all that sure that he was telling the truth. He *assumed* she would want to get married – but who knew for sure?

"Are you sure you aren't going to tell me you have some dangerous new assignment? You're not going to test some crazy new rocket or something, are you?"

"No," he said quickly. "It's not a crazy rocket." In his mind he added: *It's crazier than even that.*

The waiter delivered an especially generous slice of sweet blueberry pie topped with an ample dollop of whipped cream. The whole dessert looked like it was the size of a small row-boat.

Daniel's mind was in a jumble – and he certainly wasn't hungry. Wearily he picked up his fork and ate fast, deciding it was better to get the whole thing over with as quickly as possible. It took him just twenty-six

24

seconds to reduce the pie and cream to a mushy, sweet mess.

"Mmm," he said, trying to keep the nausea out of his voice. "That was great."

Helen jumped up and kissed him on the cheek. "I'm sorry, Danny, but I have to go."

"That's okay," Daniel said with a resigned shrug.

"I'll call you later," she said, turning toward the door.

Daniel watched her go, and then, at the last possible minute, he dashed across the restaurant, grabbed her by the arm and pulled her into the phone booth, folding the door closed behind them.

"Danny! What are you doing?"

"Are you sure you gotta go?"

"Are you sure you're okay?" She studied his face closely, searching for an answer in his eyes. The world was in such turmoil these days. There was war in Europe. Who knew what the future held for a flier like Daniel McCormick.

"I'm fine," said Danny. "I'm not planning on doing anything that'll get me killed. That's a promise."

A surprised, sweet smile broke across Helen's face. Suddenly, she could sense what was on his mind; she knew exactly what he wanted to say but couldn't find the words.

"What is it? What's on your mind, Danny?"

Danny took a deep breath and licked his lips. "I . . ." He felt his nerve breaking. "Let's never leave this phone booth, okay?"

Helen laughed. "You're acting nuts."

"It's your perfume. It's driving me crazy."

Helen pulled herself off his lap and slid the door open.

"I'll see you later."

Daniel watched her go and then banged his head against the metal side of the phone. "Stupid! Damn!"

He dropped a dime in the slot and dialed a number quickly.

"Harry? I almost did it, you know? You inspired me, but it was just . . . I couldn't get past my throat. The words, they got stuck somewhere."

Daniel paid no attention to the sounds around him. The screech of brakes and a muffled thud from the street outside penetrated the phone booth.

"Did you just come out and ask Blanche out of the blue? Or did you plan it out? 'Cause it feels like I've done it in my head two hundred times. Two hundred times I've asked her, and I still don't know what her answer will be."

Just then the door of the phone booth swept open.

"Danny." It was the waiter.

"I'll be off in a second, Tommy."

"Danny," said the waiter, his voice sick and hollow. "You better come outside."

It took Daniel a full five seconds to realize that something dreadful had happened. Suddenly he was on his feet, sprinting for the street, heading for a knot of people on the corner. He pushed through the crowd and saw Helen lying on the sidewalk, a car resting on the curb.

"I didn't see her," said a distraught man. He was twisting the brim of his hat in his hands over and over again. "I swear to God, I didn't see her. I swear to God . . ."

"Helen . . ."

Daniel felt a wave of dizziness wash over him, and

his muscles and joints seemed to go slack, as if no longer up to the task of keeping him standing upright. He tottered a few steps, then slowly sank to his knees next to Helen's broken body. He took her hand in his. It was cold.

Far in the distance a siren could be heard.

Daniel sat next to Helen's hospital bedside for six hours straight until a nurse led him away and forced him to go home. He didn't remember the drive back to his house. The only image he could see was Helen's cold gray skin, her unseeing eyes, the bandages and stitches. The only thing he could hear was the word the doctor had said: coma . . .

CHAPTER SIX

The next few weeks were the hardest of Daniel's life. Time passed in a daze of torment. Day after day he spent hours at the hospital, keeping a silent vigil at Helen's bedside, watching her for the slightest sign of recovery. But there was nothing. The bruises faded, the cuts healed, the broken bones knit and mended, but there was not a single glimmer of life in her.

The doctors and nurses, as well as Daniel's colleagues at the base, talked to him, all of them stressing the importance of normality, of getting back to his routine, of going on with his life.

After such lectures Daniel would nod and agree and swear that he would sit up and fly straight. But then he would go home, miserable and alone, staring into the gathering darkness, trying to will himself into unconsciousness.

Gradually Daniel began to unravel. He stopped shaving, then bathing. His house became a pile of garbage: overflowing ashtrays, dirty plates and empty bottles. Half-eaten meals congealed on the stove. Daniel had not been at work for weeks.

Harry decided that it was time to do something before Daniel sank into such a deep depression that it would become an enervating despondency from which he might never emerge. He knocked and tapped on the windows, peering in at the disarray in the modest house, sure that he could see Danny sitting in the gloom. "Goddammit, Danny! I know you're in there. So open the door, would ya?"

Daniel heard his friend's voice but did not react. He remained motionless in the armchair in the living room. He didn't even move a muscle when Harry put his shoulder to the door and beat his way into the filthy room.

There was an untidy pool of letters on the floor just inside the door, left just where it had fallen.

Harry rubbed his shoulder and looked around him. "I see you've cleaned up." He shook his head slowly when he looked at his friend. Daniel's hair was long, dirty and unkempt, his chin grizzled with three days' worth of whiskers. His skin was sallow except for the dark, bruised-looking ovals under his bloodshot eyes. His lips were chapped and blistered.

"Hi, Harry." Daniel stirred himself just enough to light a cigarette. He tossed the match in the general direction of an ashtray and missed. Harry leaned against the wall, then slid down until he was sitting on the floor.

"Danny, you have to snap out of it. You're killing yourself. It's like you're committing suicide."

Danny did not appear to have heard. He drew heavily on his cigarette, sucking the smoke down into his lungs and holding it there until it burned.

Harry sighed heavily. "The first two weeks they said she wouldn't wake up. That was . . . that was almost six months ago now."

"Doctors can be wrong," said Daniel. His voice was low and rough. It had been coarsened to a croak by weeks of heavy cigarette smoking and stress.

Harry shook his head. "I talked to Doctor Morrison.

And Kelvin. And Hastings and Collins. They all say the same thing, Danny."

Daniel continued to stare straight ahead. "She said, 'I'll see you later.' That was the last thing she said." He drew on the cigarette again.

"Danny, I have to tell you . . ." Harry put a hand on his friend's shoulder. "They are moving her on Tuesday. It's a chronic-care facility. In Santa Rosa. It's, uh, it's a better place, I think. The doctors say there's just nothing left they can do for her here."

If Harry hoped that his words had gotten through to Daniel, he was to be disappointed. Daniel was silent a long time. The cigarette burned between his fingers, a thin plume of smoke spiraling up into the middle of the room. "We'd play at the lighthouse. And she'd say we'd grow old there . . . together . . . in that perfect house just down the road. Harry, I don't have one memory without her. I swear, nothing was real until she knew . . ."

"Danny, everyone at the base wants to see you." Harry pointed to the pile of letters just inside the broken front door. "Those are the knocks at your door, all the letters. They're from people who care about you."

"I couldn't do it . . ."

"Sure you could."

"I couldn't do it. I couldn't ask her."

"But she knew what you felt."

Very slowly, Daniel shook his head. "Could you picture me a father?"

"Danny, you have to stop torturing yourself . . ."

"I thought I had all the time in the world. I thought *we* had all the time in the world. And I was wrong."

Harry spoke firmly. "Listen. The guys at the base, they just want to see you again. You gotta get out of here. You don't even have a door anymore."

There was a flicker of life on Daniel's rumpled face. "I don't want to see them. Don't tell them that. But it's the truth."

He took a last puff from the cigarette end and then ground it out in the overflowing ashtray. Immediately he reached for his pack and quickly lit another.

"So now what? You're just gonna become a hermit? That's not like you."

Daniel shrugged. "Let me be, would you?"

Harry could see that the direct approach was not working, that he couldn't shock Daniel back on to the path back to the land of the living. He decided that a change in strategy was called for.

"Hey, did you hear that Charlie was canned from the project? They found two bottles of gin in his locker. He tried to deny they were his, but it turns out he was so sozzled he just fell on his ass and passed out. Six days before we do the next test on the prototype and now he's out. His timing has always been great like that, right?"

Daniel hardly stirred during the telling of this sad tale, but he did show a glimmer of interest in the decline and fall of his erstwhile colleague.

"It's blue file," said Harry. "None of the brass knows about this. So, I'm gonna freeze a human being. Well, if you call Charlie a human being."

Daniel raised his eyebrows. "Charlie? How long are you going to put him under for?"

"A year. See, the beautiful thing about Charlie is that he has no life. He'll take a year off, and he won't

31

miss a thing except a couple of cases of gin. And it's a great way for me to iron out the kinks, right?"

A snapshot, painful in its clarity, appeared in Daniel's mind. He could see Helen in her hospital bed, still and lifeless. He could see the drab hospital room, the dismal corridors peopled with the sick and the lame. It was a hopeless place, despondent and full of despair. To think of Helen, the love of his life, in a place like that was to picture slow death, a wasting melancholy that he could not endure.

Harry could sense a change in his friend. "Why don't you get yourself cleaned up, Danny? She wouldn't want you to go on like this. Do it for Helen."

"No," said Daniel. "I have a better idea."

"There's a better idea than rejoining the human race?" Harry looked puzzled.

"Yeah. Don't freeze Charlie. Freeze me."

"Danny, for God's sake!"

"You don't understand, Harry."

"I understand," said Harry, his voice tinged with anger. "I understand that you have got to get a grip on yourself."

"You don't understand," said Daniel wearily.

Harry's small store of anger had been used up. "I understand. Why don't you come and stay with us for a while? We'd like that. Blanche would love it."

"Harry, I can't watch her die. I want to sleep. I want to go to sleep for a year."

"Look," said Harry sympathetically, "you've been through a lot, but there's no reason to check out of life."

"Harry, I've thought this through."

"Forget it," said Harry flatly. "Just forget all about it, okay?"

"I've been in the service for twelve years."

"Danny, I won't listen to this nonsense. For one thing, you're valuable. You're needed on the B-25 project. You can't just give that up. I never should have brought it up. The whole idea is silly. You're gonna end up making me wish I hadn't even started this damn thing."

"Forget the B-25 prototype," Daniel snapped. "There are ten guys as good as, or better than, I am. I won't be missed."

Daniel reached out and seized Harry with both arms, holding him tight as if, through touch, Daniel could communicate his pain, as if he could make Harry feel his torment for himself. Never before had Daniel tried so hard to get a point across, to let someone know how he really felt. Only with Helen had he been so open and so honest.

"Harry, I'm military. I'm healthy. I've got no family. I have nowhere to go. I know tests, I know experiments – it's my *job*. I'm perfect for this thing – you know that." He stared hard into his friend's eyes. "*Harry, let me do it*. I can't even think anymore. Please. Until it's over, let me go. I want to do it. Please."

"But," said Harry, "like you said, doctors can be wrong. That's true, you know."

"Then, if she gets better, wake me up."

Both men felt hopeless, bereft, paralyzed with grief and torment. Tears came to Daniel's eyes and dribbled down his cheeks. "Please, Harry, it's the only chance I've got right now. Please help me fight the pain."

CHAPTER SEVEN

Harry had not designed his contraption with esthetics in mind. It was an ugly, hand-made, prototype miracle, lit by the sterile lights of an operating theater. The apparatus was a jerry-rigged collection of tubes and wires, copper vats, valves and pumps. In the middle of the mechanism was the most important piece of equipment, a coffin-shaped copper capsule connected to the coolant chambers. Daniel was inside.

Outside the lab Harry had a reputation for clumsiness; he was seen as the archetypal absent-minded professor. Once inside his laboratory, his domain, he was all business. He had almost managed to forget that his best friend was now inside his device, the first human guinea pig in the untried process. He was captain of the ship, his two assistants reacting instantly to his commands.

"Bring the internal to twenty."

"Yessir!" One assistant gradually reduced the temperature within the chamber. "We're stay for phase three."

"Cancel pulse," ordered Harry. "Negative reading."

There was a loud hiss of escaping steam as the temperature within the capsule began to plummet. Within the unit all activity in Daniel's body was slowing down, like a car rolling to a halt. His pulse and heart rate were winding down; his blood was sluggish and torpid in his veins. His mind was fading out of the present and casting itself backward in time.

He saw himself at age eleven, playing on the bluffs by the lighthouse at Point Reyes, running and jumping like a young colt, Helen at his side. He could almost hear the pound of the surf in his ears, taste the salt spray in the air. He and Helen always played at the base of the lighthouse. It was their favorite place in the whole world. It was where they planned to live one day, in the old lightkeeper's house perched on the cliff. Now that only existed in his dreams.

Harry's voice sounded remote, far off and faint. "Twenty. Do we have that?"

"Copy," answered his assistant. "Phase four power descent. We have that."

A new memory seeped into Daniel's mind. He was older. Helen was older too. It was the day of their graduation from high school back in 1927. He remembered running to her, finding her in the crowd of students and catching her in his arms. In sheer exuberance he lifted her off the ground and twirled her in the air. She was laughing. He could hear her laughing.

"Reduce pressure," said Harry. "Heart rate?"

"Looking good, looking good. Venting secure. Readings are level."

A cloud of steam blew from the valves, and the temperature in the capsule dropped. The blood was thick in his veins, and the last memory was dim, hazy like a faded photograph in an old album of memories.

He and Helen were lying side by side on a blanket in a field, the remains of a picnic scattered on the grass around them. Daniel hiked himself up on one elbow and kissed her. He remembered that day as if it was only yesterday. It was as if he could still feel the warm wind on his face, the smell of the wild flowers and the scent of her perfume.

"At fourteen," said Harry, "hit the valve."

"Needle at six. Needle at six point five."

As the capacitors kicked in, the laboratory was filled with the strident whine of machinery.

"We're in the black," said Harry's assistant.

"Record time and date," Harry ordered.

"November 26th, 1939. Zero-four seventeen hundred hours," intoned Harry's subordinate.

"All right. This is it, folks. This is history."

There was another blast of steam and the screech of machinery working at top power.

Very clearly, over the roar of the equipment, Daniel heard Helen speak.

"I love you," she said.

Daniel struggled to reply but his lips did not work. His mouth seemed sewn shut. Hot waves of frustration overwhelmed him as he fought to speak. Then a great black breaker of cold time washed over him, and all was as silent, dark and cold as a crypt.

PART TWO

CHAPTER EIGHT

Never before in Nat's eleven years on earth had he attended a funeral. He found the process interesting, if a bit mystifying. The deceased, Mr Carlin, a teacher at Nat's junior high school, had died a few days before, and the entire student body, teachers and staff of the San Marco Junior High School had turned out to attend the final rites of one of their own.

The principal of the school, Mrs Rose, sobbed through the service, almost drowning out the words of the priest who intoned as the coffin was slowly lowered into the grave.

Nat felt like he was intruding on her grief, and he looked away, staring at the sky, and was delighted when an X-29 experimental aircraft from the local air base streaked across the sky.

The X-29 was one of the strangest-looking planes in the United States Air Force of the 1990s. Its wings were swept forward – it looked like a plane flying backward – and the entire powerful machine was under the control of a computer, the pilot more or less along for the ride. It was said that if the computer malfunctioned, the X-29 would plummet, which must have made things exciting for the man in the cockpit.

The aircraft was gone in a second, but the funeral dragged on and on until Nat thought it would never end. He spent the rest of the service watching a girl from his class called Alice – Nat had a crush on her, but he would have died if she knew. He hardly ever spoke to her, but he was in love with her from afar. She did not seem to know he was alive.

Eventually the funeral concluded, and rather than return the students for the rump end of a school day, they were allowed to take the rest of the day off.

Nat and his best friend Felix rode their bikes back to Nat's house and clambered up into their treehouse. Both boys were connoisseurs of junk food, and they kept a small supply of assorted candies and cakes in this, their fortress. They both selected Hostess Twinkies and unwrapped them reverently, like wine lovers sampling a rare vintage from a great cellar.

The two had different tactics in eating. Nat was straightforward in his attack, Felix a little more subtle. Nat ate his in a normal manner. Felix had a little ritual that he was compelled to perform. First he sucked the powerfully sweet "cream" out of the tube of the cake, then he broke it, stuck it on his thumb and nibbled around the edges nervously.

"What's up?" asked Nat after a while.

"Nothing much. Got to go to the dentist tomorrow."

"Oooh, boy."

Felix flinched. "Tell me about it."

"Want to eat at my house tonight?" asked Nat.

"Nope."

"Don't blame you."

Nat's mother Claire was not famous for her skills in the kitchen, and it was with something approximating dread that Nat waited for the dinner hour. When it finally came and Felix had departed for his own home Nat, resigned to another inedible meal, took his place at the table in the kitchen facing their dinner guest.

John was a special friend of his mother's, a big bear of a man with a thick beard and smiling eyes. He was better at concealing his distaste for Claire's cuisine than Nat.

"Any good?" Claire asked, watching John. Claire was in her thirties. She was pretty, not glamorous or dazzling, just pretty. She had done everything within her means to make her modest home comfortable, but her talents did not extend to the kitchen.

"Yum," said John.

"Nat?"

"Great," said Nat without enthusiasm.

Claire smiled. "Better be. I cooked it a special, top-secret way, just for you. Cost a hell of a lot more."

Nat looked at his mother for a moment, and it was plain from the expression on his face that he was wondering if his mother had completely lost her mind.

"Fine," she said, "don't believe me."

John put down his fork. "When does your summer camp start, Nat?"

"Couple of weeks. It's Boy Scout camp."

John smiled. "I remember camp. I remember my counselor carried a first-aid kit. That white box, with the red cross, the way it closed with this *click*. That's why I wanted to be a doctor. That click."

"You became a doctor because of a click on a first-aid kit?" asked Claire.

"That's right."

"That's really strange. Don't you think that's really strange, Nat?"

"No," said Nat. "Not really."

"Looking forward to going?" asked John.

Nat shrugged. "I guess."

"Got your uniform yet?"

"Oops," said Claire. "That is a touchy subject."

"Not yet." Nat turned and looked hard at his mother disapprovingly.

"I promise, next week at the latest. He thinks all his sizes are gonna be sold out, and he'll end up looking like a geek. Right?"

At that moment the sore subject of Boy Scout uniforms was not much on Nat's mind. He was more concerned about the funeral he had attended that day.

"Mrs Rose wouldn't stop crying. She said she was okay, but she kept crying like she couldn't help it. I didn't cry. I didn't know Mr Carlin. I would have had him next year."

Claire and John exchanged a quick glance. It was apparent that Nat was confused, maybe a little upset, and was grappling with the events of the day, trying to come to terms with what he had witnessed.

Claire stroked her son's hair. "Mr Carlin was real old. And he was a teacher for a long time."

"What happens when you die?" Nat asked bluntly.

"Well . . ." Claire thought for a moment. "It's sort of like when you're asleep. It's very peaceful. Almost like a dream."

"Felix says you rot."

"Well, uh," Claire shot an imploring glance at John, begging for a little assistance. This was much closer to his specialty than hers.

John cleared his throat. "See, Nat, what happens is your body becomes part of the earth again. That helps trees grow and trees help people to live . . . and so, in a way, you never really die at all."

Nat thought this through, and he seemed to be satisfied. He went back to picking at his food.

At the end of the meal Claire walked John to the door. She was glad he had come over for dinner, but she was also glad he was going early. She was dead tired and it showed in her eyes.

"You were good company," she said.

"She said, yawning," John filled in.

"I'm not yawning."

"You were about to."

Claire yawned and laughed at the same time. "Sorry about dinner. I tend to burn things."

"No, no, it wasn't really burnt. It was just well done. In fact, it was significantly, dramatically well done."

Claire laughed again. She was used to jokes about her cooking, and they had long since stopped bothering her.

"Let's do it again," said John.

"Any time. We can always get a table. I know the maitre d'."

"It's good to have friends in high places." He turned toward the street. "I'll see you at the hospital."

When Claire tucked Nat in for the night she could see that he was still troubled slightly. She did all she could to reassure him.

"*You* are a bright, gorgeous, healthy kid. With wonderful ideas and dreams and a long, long life to look forward to. And, just so you know, I'm not going anywhere."

"Good," he said in a very small voice.

"And, listen, if you *ever* feel confused or anything, talk to me. Got that?"

"Uh-huh."

"Promise?"

"Promise," said Nat.

Claire smoothed the blankets on the bed and then bent and kissed her son tenderly on the forehead.

"And we've got the air show this weekend, right?" There were airplane posters plastered on the walls of Nat's bedroom. Models and books on aviation took up a lot of space in the room.

"Uh-huh. You know, you can invite John. If you want to."

Claire was touched by her son's attempt to bring a man into her life. "Maybe I will. Goodnight."

"Goodnight, Mom." Nat hiked himself up on his elbows. "And you know what?"

Claire stopped at the door. "What?"

"It wasn't burned too bad this time."

CHAPTER NINE

Felix had an older brother, Steven, and, like most older brothers, Steven was Felix's waking nightmare. He was bigger and stronger, of course, and he considered himself to be supremely cool mainly because he was eighteen and in the Air Force Reserve. Once a week he got dressed up in his uniform and went out to the base and mostly got ordered around by men who were not in the reserves but in the Air Force proper. But from Nat's and Felix's point of view, Steven dwelled on the highest pinnacle of a towering military Olympus.

Steven was particularly nightmarish right now, as Felix's parents had gone to Las Vegas on their second honeymoon and Steven was in charge of the house. It was also Steven's Air Force Reserve day, so, instead of driving Felix directly home from the dentist (Nat having gone along to lend moral support), they drove out to the airbase. Steven, of course, neglected to tell his passengers about this slight deviation from plan.

Steven drove his old Dodge out to the base and pulled up next to an enormous warehouse. A military moving crew was working in the warehouse. Four giant industrial moving trucks growled in and out of the building, and men in olive drab fatigues were busy loading crates on to flat-bed trucks. Electric forklifts whirred through the confusion, stacking boxes on palette jacks.

"Hey," said Felix, "what's going on? What's this?" His speech was a little indistinct, muffled as it was by the dental cotton that had been packed into his mouth.

"It's called *parking*," said Steven as he carefully positioned his car between the white parking lines.

"I thought you were taking us home."

"Chill out, freak," Steven snapped. "I'm dropping something off. Unlike you, I've got *responsibilities*."

"Mom said you were gonna take us home. Directly home, she said."

"You know, Felix, that's a great story. But Mom and Dad are in Las Vegas, and I'm not." He pulled a sheaf of official-looking papers from the glove compartment and then turned and stared malevolently at the two boys in the back seat.

"You move from this car . . ."

"Yeah?"

"You move from this car and one day . . . maybe ten years from now . . . when you're least expecting it, your guard is down . . . I'll put a poisonous snake in your bed." He pointed to Nat. "The same goes for you."

Steven got out of the car and walked quickly into the warehouse. Nat and Felix watched him go.

"Nice guy," said Nat.

"A prince," said Felix.

Steven marched up to the nearest officer, a captain, saluted and proffered the papers. "Additional work orders, sir. As you requested, sir."

The captain glanced at the papers for a little longer than half a second. Right at that moment he wanted no part of additional work orders. He had plenty of work right here. So, in keeping with fine military tradition, he passed the buck to an inferior.

"Go see Lieutenant Church," he said, handing the papers back. "He's in the office round the back."

"Yessir," said Steven with a snappy salute.

Lieutenant Church was on the phone, and he stayed on the phone for a very long time. When he finally got off the phone, being no less a respecter of military tradition, he told Steven that he had come to the wrong place.

"You want Sergeant Samuels. He's in the trailer out front, by the loading dock."

Steven, a good soldier, did exactly what he was told.

Felix and Nat stared intently at the digital clock set in the dashboard of Steven's car. It read 11:45.

"It's been twenty-six minutes," said Nat.

"Twenty-seven minutes and fifteen seconds," droned Felix. "Sixteen seconds . . . seventeen seconds . . . eighteen seconds . . ."

Suddenly Nat had a very bright idea. "Let's pretend we're dead."

"Okay."

Both boys fell back against the car seat, assuming looks of suggested sudden and violent death, their eyes bugging out, tongues lolling out of their mouths. This was fun for just under five seconds.

"This is getting lame," said Nat.

The warehouse looked far more inviting. The two boys wandered into the darkness and the clutter. There were acres of military paraphernalia, the kind of junk that builds up over decades: desks, filing cabinets, machinery, bunks and footlockers. The moving crew plainly had its work cut out for it, and it was still on the far side of the warehouse, a long way from Nat and Felix. The vast building seemed to stretch endlessly into the gloom.

47

"Wow," said Nat in awe. "This place is *big*."

"Race you to the end?"

"Yeah!"

Both boys were off and running, sprinting for the wall deep inside the warehouse, their footsteps echoing in the darkness.

The race ended in a dead heat, more or less, but neither boy really cared about the outcome. They had run a thousand races during the course of their friendship, and they had realized one thing: sometimes Nat won, other times Felix was the victor.

The terrain in the very back of the warehouse was fascinating – a maze of dusty boxes and bales, a cornucopia of bewitching junk.

Felix examined one of the barrels closely. It was wrapped in electrical wires.

"Wow! A bomb!"

Both boys knew that it wasn't a *real* bomb, but for the purposes of play, the barrel became one.

"Yeah," said Nat. "And we have to defuse it!"

"Right!" Felix looked at the maze of wires. "Cut the blue wire."

"You sure?"

"Absolutely."

Nat pantomimed snipping the wire, using his fingers as scissors. Suddenly his eyes grew wide in horror.

"Booooom!" he shouted, hurling himself back as if thrown by the force of the explosion. He tumbled to the floor, writhing and flailing his arms. "Help! I'm on fire!"

"I'll put you out!" Felix pulled a can of silly string from his pocket like a gunslinger and blasted the sticky, ropy strands all over the human torch.

But suddenly Nat wasn't playing along. He was staring into the murky recesses of the warehouse.

"Hey, man, you burned bad?" asked Felix.

"What *is* that thing?" Nat got to his feet and pointed. Nestling at the back of the warehouse was the capsule, Harry's capsule. It was rusted and covered in layers of dust and cobwebs, beneath which was a thick coat of black soot. It was dented and scratched, but there was something inherently gripping about the object.

Nat had no idea what it was but he was drawn to it, mesmerized by the weird object.

"I think it's part of a submarine," said Felix with an air of authority.

"In the Air Force?"

"That's why it's here. They figured they didn't need it, so they junked it."

"That makes sense."

They circled the capsule warily, taking in the tangle of pipes and valves that were attached to it. Nat wiped the grime from one of the gauges.

"The needle says . . . sixty-five."

"Sixty-five what?"

"*I* dunno."

"I'll bet it's sixty-five feet. Periscope depth. Ready to raise periscope."

Nat immediately threw himself into the game. He turned one of the valves. "Roger. Periscope up!"

Felix clambered on to the top of the capsule, like a captain on the bridge.

"Oh, no! We have a leak!"

"Emergency!" shouted Nat. He fell on one large valve and yanked, turning the wheel around and around. Suddenly the capsule started hissing, quietly at first, but as the coolant escaped in greater volume, the sound level increased. Both boys looked at each other and paled.

"Hey . . ."

The top section of the contraption shifted suddenly, throwing Felix to the dirty floor. The air around the apparatus suddenly turned cold, and Nat shivered inside his jacket.

"Nat," said Felix, "I think we better . . ."

"Take a closer look?"

"Yeah!"

The two boys struggled to raise the lid of the device. The hinges squeaked, and the metal groaned as the rust cracked and twisted.

The inside of the mechanism was just as interesting as the exterior. The interior was shiny and coppery, molded perfectly to fit an icy blue-gray plastic sack. Cold air billowed out of the capsule. Felix reached in, groping at the sides of the capsule.

"Careful," cautioned Nat.

Felix brushed his fingers across the top of the bag. "It's cold," he said. He grabbed the zipper on the side of the pouch and tugged on it, pulling it down to reveal a cloth covering, code numbers stenciled on the outer edge. Nat looked nervous.

Quickly Felix unlaced the top of the second bag and tore at it, yanking vigorously. After a bit of a struggle, he tugged away enough material to reveal the head of a man. There were silver-foil patches over his eyes, and there were plugs in his ears. It was Daniel.

Nat's and Felix's mouths dropped open, and their eyes grew as wide as dinner plates.

"Wow!" gasped Felix.

Given eleven-year-old boys' profound interest in the dead, grotesque, weird and deformed, the sight of Daniel had to be counted as the most sublime moment in the short lives of Nat and Felix.

Nat found his voice, peering in closely at the figure. "Think he's . . . dead?"

"I don't know. He sure does look terrible!"

"I think he's dead," said Nat flatly.

In that instant Daniel's chest heaved as he took a deep, intense breath. His arm shot out and grabbed Nat in an icy grasp.

Everything seemed to happen at once. Both boys screamed, and Felix fell to the floor. The dental cotton in his mouth shot out like a wadded bullet. Nat was crying and struggling to get free of the hand of the monster. Felix jumped to his feet and grabbed at Nat, trying to haul him away from the capsule. Nat squirmed out of his jacket, leaving it in Daniel's frigid clutch. The two boys raced out of the warehouse and dove into the back seat of the car.

Steven slipped in behind the wheel a moment later. "Now that didn't take so long, did it?"

Felix was almost bouncing off the walls of the car. "Steven! We went inside! There was this thing!" He was babbling almost incoherently. There was nothing more likely to annoy his brother. "A big metal thing and it opened up and there was a dead guy and he grabbed Nat and he's still in there!"

Steven started the engine of the car. "Listen. *Shut up!*"

"Steven," said Nat frantically. "I *swear*. He was really cold! And he grabbed me and took my jacket. He's still got it. In there." Nat pointed to the warehouse.

51

"Hey, if I was cold, I'd take your jacket too. You are both pathetic. You know that?"

"It was real," insisted Felix.

"Be quiet. Now *I*'m the boss in this car. Me. I am. And the boss says shut up. Any questions?"

There were no questions from Nat and Felix.

"Good," said Steven.

CHAPTER TEN

Dinner that night was, as usual, cooked on the well-done side of the spectrum, but neither Felix nor Nat really noticed what they were eating. Their initial terror of their experience had worn off, replaced by an immeasurable curiosity and a delicious sense that they had been a whisper away from danger and had escaped without a scratch. Nat wondered if he would have a nightmare about the dead guy that night.

Claire was sceptical, the way a mother was supposed to be, but she couldn't shake Nat's and Felix's story of a brush with a frozen maniac.

"You *sure* this isn't just the finest excuse you've ever come up with for losing a jacket?" she asked, her eyes narrowing, drawing a bead on her son.

Nat had to agree. "Yeah, it'd be a great excuse, but, no, it's *true*. This frozen guy was *there*."

"I saw him too, Mrs Cooper," said Felix. "I saw him too. I was there."

"Well, I'm sure that gentleman's in there for a reason. Besides, your name and address are in the jacket – if someone finds it maybe they'll return it. Pass the peas, would you, Felix?"

Of course, when it came right down to it, Claire thought that the two boys were just the victims of their own over-heated imaginations. Maybe they really did believe they had seen something strange out at the base, but Claire knew, with the reasoning of an adult, that they had not.

In the hours since the boys had discovered him, Daniel had slowly, erratically, come back to life. His body temperature was on the rise, and his cells were beginning to thaw. He knew he was alive – every muscle, sinew and organ in his body was aflame with pain – but that was all he knew. Convulsions were detonating in his guts, sending blinding blasts of pain through his body, and he opened his mouth to scream in anguish, but no sound came.

Shaking uncontrollably, he grasped the side of the copper capsule and kicked his way out of the cloth shrouds that he had been wrapped in for so many years. His brain sent messages to his limbs, but, as if there was static on the line, the bulletin did not get through clearly. As he tried to climb out of the capsule he lost his balance, tumbled to the floor and sprawled there, naked and shivering.

His breathing was hard and labored, and for a moment he did not think he would have the strength to stand. Slowly, hand over hand, he hauled himself up, clawing his way up the side of the capsule until he stood, unsteadily, on his feet.

He found Nat's jacket and, with immense effort, managed to tie the garment around his waist. Then he began to walk, stumbling through the maze of crates and barrels, moving only inches at a time. His eyes were fast recovering, adjusting to the gloom, looking around. He was terrified.

Through a foggy haze a jumble of memories, a single clear thought, emerged: *Harry! He had to find Harry!*

At first the open window in the warehouse wall looked about as attainable as the summit of Mount

Everest, but Daniel knew he had to climb up to it and escape. Laboriously he clambered up a precipice of crates, grasped the window sill and pulled himself out into the cool night air. He hung there for a moment, then dropped to the concrete apron outside the warehouse.

Daniel crouched on the pavement for a moment, a low moan escaping from his lips. He shivered in the darkness and stared up at the night sky.

He stumbled across the air base, leaving the purely military portion of the complex and wandering into the housing area. In the moonlight he could make out laundry flapping in the wind, drying on a clothesline. As Daniel drew nearer he saw that the only clothing on the line, among a great waft of sheets and towels, was a white women's uniform blouse and a pair of green sweat shorts. Quickly he tore them from the line and put them on, but he kept the jacket, not wanting to leave any trace of his having been there. Then he set off, wandering out into the night.

He was on the highway now, terrified and confused by the traffic that roared by him. The low sleekness of the cars, the giant trucks – they were unlike anything he had seen before. Where had they come from? Were these behemoths prototypes, secret projects under development in this remote part of California? But there were so many of them, too many to keep secret.

His mind awhirl, he stumbled down the highway toward the bright lights on the horizon. The cluster of lights was a Ralph's mini-market, a pool of brightness in the dark night. In the parking lot was a phone booth, a strange, high-tech-looking contraption.

Daniel snatched the receiver off the hook and looked bewildered at the face of the instrument. Where the rotor dial should have been there were twelve buttons. For a moment the whole process was beyond him. He was incapable of doing something as simple as making a phone call. Then, with a rush of relief, he saw that "O" still connected you with an operator.

"Nine-three-eight. Can I help you?"

Daniel opened his mouth to speak, but the only sound he could emit was a strangled, stuttering whisper.

"May I help you?"

"I . . . ahhh . . . uhhhh."

"Hello?" The operator did not sound as if she was in a mood to be trifled with.

Daniel growled and coughed, trying to clear his throat. Finally he was able to force some air through his larynx. His voice was uncertain and broke like a teenager's.

"Hello?" He managed to utter.

"Sir," said the operator sharply, "I can barely hear you. Is this an emergency?"

Damn right it's an emergency, thought Daniel. "Y-y-yes. P-p-please." From the recesses of his addled brain he managed to dredge up Harry's phone number. "Richmond . . . tthhree-ffour-ttwo."

The effort required to gasp out these four words nearly drained him of all his strength.

"Excuse me?" snapped the operator.

Please, thought Daniel, *don't make me say it again*.

"I did not hear the number, sir."

Daniel filled his lungs. "Richmond . . . three . . . four . . . two." To his surprise, he found that the effort

56

required to speak was not nearly as immense as the time before.

The operator hesitated. "The exchange is Richmond?"

"Y-yes."

"Then three-four-two?"

"Yes."

"Seven-four-three-four-two?"

"Yes," stammered Daniel. "H-Harry Finley. P-please. Please . . ."

"Sir," said the operator, "you're missing two digits."

"T-two digits?"

"Yes. You need seven digits. You only gave me five. You need seven."

"But —"

"Please check the number and dial again," said the operator as if she was no more human than a machine. Then she hung up.

Daniel sighed heavily and looked around him. There was a banner strung over the parking lot of the Ralph's. Daniel stared at it for a moment, not quite able to believe his eyes: 'Wings of Freedom Air Show 1992'.

Terror flooded through him. Tears sprang into his eyes. "Oh, brother," he muttered.

CHAPTER ELEVEN

Not long after dawn Daniel stumbled up the access road to the air base, making directly for the guard booth at the main gate. The nineteen-year-old private on duty had spent a long, boring night guarding the gate, and he did not need any trouble now just as his shift was due to come to an end.

He stared hard at the plainly demented character staggering toward him and quietly snapped open the cuff of his holster. He had never fired a shot in anger, and he wasn't sure he could actually bring himself to use his gun if he had to, but it was nice to know it was there.

Daniel was trying to ignore the soldier, strolling toward the gate as if he had a perfect right to be there.

"Hold it," said the guard. "Let's hold it right there, okay?"

"I-I-I'm looking for a friend of mine. H-he's stationed here."

"Okay, sir. You give me his name. I'll call him up. He'll have to come out here and get you, okay?" Once a year every soldier stationed on the base had to attend a seminar on sensitivity and dealing with civilians. It was always impressed on the attendees that you had to be slavishly polite to those not in uniform, even unbalanced, homeless people like this guy the guard was now confronted with.

"T-that's fine."

"And his name is . . .?"

"Harry Finley," said Daniel.

"Okay." The guard took out the base directory and leafed through it. "Lessee . . . Farmer, Farrell, Finletter, Finman. Sorry. No Finley. Uh, no one stationed here with that name, sir."

Daniel closed his eyes for a moment. Where was Harry? This was beginning to feel like a nightmare that would never come to an end.

"Th-then I n-need to talk t-to someone else . . . in ch-charge."

"Uh-huh. Look, what's this about exactly?"

"It's c-classified."

The kid nodded to himself. *Of course it's classified. Nuts always have some kind of secret information.* "Yeah, I'm sorry, sir. But there's no way I can let you in. No way in hell, sir."

Daniel nodded and moved in closer. "I know . . . I know how I must look to you. But trust me. *Please.*"

"I'm sorry, sir. I'm going to ask you to leave these premises, sir. You are standing on government property."

Daniel sighed and nodded, and it looked as if he was going to go on his way when suddenly he seized the kid by the shirt front and threw him back against the wall of the guard booth.

"Hey! You *freak!*" It never occurred to the guard to pull his gun – he was too surprised by this unexpected development.

"My name . . . is Lieutenant . . . Daniel McCormick. 241988539. I'm s-sure . . . you're a nice kid. But if you don't get me inside . . . *now* . . . I'll see to it . . . th-that you s-stay a private . . . for the rest . . . of your military career."

There was something in Daniel's halting voice and

the look on his face that made the private think that he might just mean what he said. Instead of seeing madness in Daniel's eyes, he saw a very determined man. The young soldier had heard rumors all over the base about secret test facilities, experiments in psychological warfare, survival skills and other things like that. Maybe this "lieutenant" was the victim of some wild experiment that had flamed out.

"I'll call the officer of the guard," said the kid. "But that's all."

"Th-thank you." Daniel allowed himself the faintest glimmer of hope. It wasn't much, but it was a start, a step in the right direction.

Captain Wilcox was only a few years older than the private on the gate, and for a moment Daniel was taken aback. It seemed as if they were only taking kids in the service these days. Then he realized that he himself wasn't all that much older than the young captain. He just *felt* a lot older.

Captain Wilcox was serious and somber, listening carefully to Daniel's strange tale and all the while taking notes on a pad of paper.

"I kn-know this must sound very strange to you," said Daniel nervously. He rearranged the jacket that was lying in his lap.

"Uh-huh." Wilcox frowned at his notes. "Let me just clarify some points. Now, you say this project was registered as Project B. Is that right?"

"R-right."

"And B stood for Buford?"

Daniel nodded. "That was the n-name of the chicken."

"The chicken that Harry Finley first froze, then thawed out."

Daniel was encouraged. This young man seemed to be taking all this quite seriously. "That is correct."

Wilcox nodded to himself. "I see." He added a detail to his notes. "And you woke up last night."

"Correct."

"Woke up last night in that old storage warehouse we are tearing down."

Daniel started to laugh. "Sounds c-c-crazy, I know, but that's the t-truth."

"Well, it is a little unusual. But this is very important. Who was your supervising officer?"

"Boyle. Colonel David E. Boyle."

"Boyle," repeated Wilcox. "David E., Colonel." He wrote this down carefully.

"I went to where Harry's house used to be, but now there's a place called Ralph's there."

"That a fact?"

"I was surprised."

"I can imagine. Well, we don't keep records here that go back to 1939, but there's a team of scientists that'll be fascinated to hear what you've got to say. And this is all very highly classified information."

Daniel nodded. "That's c-correct. Harry told no one the details. Not even the people who worked for him." He thought for a moment. "Well, there was one other person who knew something about it."

"Ah-ha," said Wilcox. "And do you have his name?"

"Her name. She's dead."

"Oh. Well. I'm going to go ahead and call the head of G-2. You know how the security people like to get in early on these things."

"That would be swell."

He considered himself lucky to have been assigned to this trusting and sober young officer. Daniel was beginning to feel much better, in both body and soul – so good, in fact, that he would not have minded a smoke.

There was a pack of cigarettes on the desk, and as Wilcox dialed he pointed to them. "Do you mind?"

"Nope. Help yourself."

Daniel examined the cigarette pack closely. "Filters? Do those things work?"

"It's just a gimmick," said Wilcox with an understanding smile.

Daniel lit the cigarette with a match and inhaled mightily, savoring the feeling of the smoke. It was familiar, a comfort, a little piece of the past.

The connection had been made, and Wilcox started talking. "Yeah, Sam, it's me. Look, I've got someone here, someone with a really interesting story." Wilcox turned slowly in his swivel chair, his clipboard in his lap. As he turned, Daniel could see what he had been writing. There were no notes, just doodles, pictures of chickens and ice cubes and faces with crazy eyes.

Daniel was stunned, shocked that this young man was humoring him, stalling for time until he could get someone to respond. And that someone was bound to have a straitjacket that would be just Daniel's size.

"Yeah, so, Sam," Wilcox continued, "I *really* think you should get over here. Bring some of your men with you, *pronto*, and deal with this *very special* situation, if you know what I mean."

He swung around in the chair and saw that Daniel had fled. The only evidence that he had ever been there was the cigarette smoldering in the ashtray.

Wilcox laughed to himself. "Hey, Sam, cancel it. Just a false alarm." He hung up and shook his head, laughing. "The nuts you get in California." Silently Wilcox awarded himself an A-plus in civilian-sensitivity training.

Daniel walked as quickly as he could toward the gate. His mind was reeling. Now what?

CHAPTER TWELVE

Nat and Felix were sprawled on the floor of Nat's living room, their eyes glued to the video game they were playing.

"I think you're lying," said Nat, skillfully manipulating the Nintendo controls. On the screen of the television set a long line of Tetris blocks slid neatly into place.

"I swear. The dentist said he had never seen so many cavities in one mouth at one time, and he wants to send a sample of my saliva to the University of Washington."

The doorbell rang, and Nat surrendered the Nintendo controls to go and answer it. "I don't believe it."

"Why would I make up a story like that?"

Nat swung open the front door of the house. Daniel stood there, looking desperate, like a lunatic in a horror movie, his hair in disarray, his eyes wild, reckless. He was clutching Nat's jacket, and he thrust it under the nose of the boy, showing him the label.

"Are you Nat Cooper?" Daniel demanded.

For a second or two Nat could only stare. He felt as if his sneakers had suddenly sent out roots deep into the ground, pinning him to the spot. His eyes grew wide, and suddenly he jumped straight up in the air, his arms waving wildly.

"*It's the dead guy!*" He ran past Felix, shrieking, charging through the house like a bullet.

It took only a split second for Felix to realize what was going on. He jumped to his feet and followed his friend, screaming at the top of his lungs.

Daniel was right after him. "I'm n-not a d-dead guy," he protested, chasing the two boys through the house.

Nat and Felix burst out of the back door of the house and ran shouting across the lawn. They were racing frantically for the treehouse, scrambling up the makeshift ladder as if their lives depended on it, as if the flimsy little structure was an indestructible fortress that Daniel would never be able to penetrate.

Nat cowered in a corner. *"He's going to kill us!"*

Daniel climbed the ladder and thrust his head into the hut. He was as spooked as the children – maybe even more so. They at least knew where they were and what the time was, and they probably had complete wardrobes.

"Don't kill us!" yelped Felix.

"Please!" screamed Nat. He squirmed on the rough boards of the treehouse as if trying to burrow through the old wooden slats.

"I'm not going to kill you!" shouted Daniel.

Felix and Nat looked decidedly unconvinced by this reassurance, bellowed at them by a scratchy-voiced lunatic.

"I'm not going to kill you," said Daniel, attempting to modulate his voice. "Okay?"

The two boys were so terrified that they could not move. They just watched as Daniel tried to calm himself down. He took a deep breath. "Okay?"

Both boys nodded. If he was going to kill them, it seemed that he would not be doing it right then. They had at least a precious five minutes of life left.

"Why do I have your jacket?" Daniel asked.

Simultaneously Nat and Felix burst into life as torrents of words tumbled from them.

"We went to the warehouse with Felix's brother Steven —"

"My brother's in the reserve, and he kept us in the car, and we got bored —"

"We were playing inside and saw this thing we thought was a submarine —"

"And we went in to find him, and we saw this thing and started climbing on it —"

"And we hit something and the top fell off —"

"Which was real stupid of us, climbing on it, and I guess somehow —"

"And Felix fell over and when we looked inside and there you were —"

"I swear the whole thing was a mistake — that's all, just a mistake —"

"Woah, woah, woah," said Daniel, throwing his hands up to protect himself from this avalanche of words. "All right. *Wait a minute!*"

Abruptly both boys stopped talking.

"Okay," said Daniel. "Just you." He pointed to Nat. 'You tell me what happened."

Nat took a deep breath. "We were playing around in there, even though we weren't supposed to, and we saw that big metal thing, and we were pretending it was a mini-sub, and we opened it up, and there you were." He turned to Felix for corroboration. "That's all, right?"

Felix nodded vigorously. "Right."

Daniel looked even more mystified. "And there were no guards? No doctors?"

"No, sir. Just a bunch of junk."

Daniel slumped against the wall of the treehouse, the information he had received beginning to sink in.

"Junk? Just junk? I have got to find Harry."

"Harry?" asked Felix.

"A friend of mine."

"Where does he live?"

"I don't know . . . not anymore."

Nat was reasonably sure that the dead guy had lost interest in killing them. "Why don't you look him up in the phone book?"

There were eight Finleys in the phone book, but Harry was not one of them.

"Guess I'll have to call them all," said Daniel, dialing the first number. "Hello, ma'am. I'm looking for a gentleman named Harry Finley. He used to live in the area, and I was hoping you might be related . . . Okay. We . . . Thanks anyway."

Daniel slammed down the phone, frustrated that his search for the elusive Harry was getting nowhere. Felix and Nat sat at the kitchen table, watching his every move.

"You kids do this a lot?"

"Do what?" asked Felix.

"Mess with classified military experiments."

Nat shook his head, a solemn expression on his face. "No, sir. This is the first time. And my name's Nat. This is Felix."

"Hi," said Felix.

"Hi," said Daniel. He consulted the phone book and started dialing again.

"What's your name?" Nat asked.

"Daniel," said Daniel. "Hello, sir . . ."

Felix examined Daniel's unorthodox taste in clothing, the torn sweat shorts and the lady's blouse. "You know, if you want, I can steal some clothes from my dad – my parents are on vacation in Las Vegas."

Daniel suddenly pulled away from the phone and looked very puzzled. "This man just told me to leave a message . . . and then he . . . squealed in my ear."

Nat grabbed the receiver from Daniel's hand. "Hi, this is Nat. I'm looking for a guy named Harry Finley. If you know how to find him, please call me at 992-4342. Thanks." He hung up. "It was just an answering machine."

Daniel looked at him incredulously. "A machine? A machine that answers phones? What the heck has happened in the last fifty years?"

"Well," said Nat, "if you want, I can show you. But you really should get some new clothes."

"Yeah," agreed Felix. "You know, in that green and white you look sorta like a Girl Scout."

CHAPTER THIRTEEN

The first stop was the library, where Daniel wanted to get a sense of the history of the last five decades.

Nat and Felix checked some microfilms out at the circulation desk and threaded them on to the viewers. They started with Pearl Harbor. The declaration of World War II did not surprise Daniel all that much – war clouds were gathering around America in 1939. Why else was the Air Corps so anxious to develop the B-25 so quickly?

"We won that one," said Nat. "But it wasn't easy."

"That one?" said Daniel. "How many wars did we have?"

"Well, there was Vietnam."

"Desert Storm," put in Felix.

"Panama."

"Grenada."

"Grenada?" said Daniel. "How did that happen?"

"I'm not sure," said Nat.

Daniel was dressed in a pair of blue jeans and a work shirt belonging to Felix's father, so he didn't look all that strange anymore, but he still had a lot to learn about the new world in which he found himself.

"How does this thing work?"

Nat showed him the controls of the microfilm reader. "Move these knobs, see?" Six months of newsprint shot across the screen. "You can forward or backward. It's easy. I used it for my history report."

Daniel hit the rewind button and he shot backward through '41 and '40 and into '39.

"So what do you do anyway?" asked Nat. "Like, for a job?"

Daniel never took his eyes off the screen. "Test pilot."

The words thrilled Nat and Felix. They stepped back from him, a gesture of respect, their mouths open. Then they started whispering frantically.

"Felix! Oh, my God!"

"He's a *pilot*!"

"We found a *pilot*!"

"Oh, my God!"

"It's the coolest thing of all time,' said Nat eagerly. "I can't believe how lucky we got!"

But something had caught Felix's eye. He tapped his friend on the shoulder. "Nat."

"What?"

"Look."

Nat turned. Alice, the love of his life, was coming into the library, a couple of books under her arm. Nat suddenly felt faint with fear. Of all the other people on earth only Felix knew Nat's deep, dark secret concerning his profound but hidden love for the lovely Alice.

"I'm in the library during summer vacation," he said in a panicked whisper to Felix. "She'll think I'm a geek."

"Nat, she's here too," said Felix with eminent good sense.

"Oh, yeah, that's right. Yeah."

Alice walked right by them. "Hi," she said.

"Hey," said Nat enthusiastically. "Hi. Hi." That

seemed to be about the extent of his conversation, but, desperate to delay her departure, he said the first thing that came into his mind. "Hey, that's bitchin' nail polish."

Alice looked at her red nails. There wasn't anything particularly outstanding about her nail polish. "Oh, thanks," she said uncertainly.

"Yeah. It's great. It looks like blood."

Alice forced herself to smile, and Nat was acutely aware of the fact that he was making a jerk of himself. Even Daniel tore his eyes away from the microfilm screen reader to stare at him for a moment.

Nat decided on another conversational gambit. "Yeah. I'm just here to do some reading." He grabbed the book nearest to him. "See. It's . . . uh . . . *Little Women*. It's great."

"Good," said Alice.

"So . . . what, your summer's going good so far and stuff? Yeah? Hey, I got into a *huge* bike accident."

"Oh, really?" said Alice politely, feigning interest.

"Major." Nat nodded emphatically. "Thrashed my bike. Thrashed. Totally thrashed. And my knee. Check it out. Look."

Quickly he yanked up his pants leg to reveal a giant scab on his bruised knee.

"Gross," said Alice.

"Yeah. Absolutely. It's a big scab, but I'm not gonna pick at it."

"Well, that's good," said Alice, a sick little smile on her pretty face.

"Yeah, thanks."

"Well," said Alice. "See you."

"Okay. Cool. 'Bye." As soon as she was out of earshot his shoulders slumped. "I'm a geek."

Felix did his best to make his friend feel better. "No, that was good. I think she likes you a lot."

"That was Alice," Nat said to Daniel. "I'm sorry I didn't introduce you. I just didn't want to hit her with too much all at once, you know?"

But Daniel didn't respond. It was as if he couldn't hear him. Nat and Felix looked at the screen and they froze too.

There was a photograph of Daniel standing on the broken wing of the B-25 he had crash-landed all those years ago. Nat and Felix looked at the picture, then at Daniel. He had not changed a bit. Next to the photo, though, was the accompanying news story. The headline: SECOND VICTIM FOUND IN LAST WEEK'S FIRE.

The two boys looked at the aircraft and the date of the newspaper.

"He's an antique pilot," said Nat.

"An antique *dead* pilot," said Felix.

"Man," said Nat, awestruck, "can you imagine reading in the paper that you're dead?"

"Yeah. What a drag that must be."

"I have to find out more," whispered Daniel. "I have to find Harry."

Daniel couldn't think of anywhere else to go but the Civil Records Division at City Hall. It was a small office in the hall of records, presided over by a young woman who listened to Daniel's plight sympathetically but was unable to do much to help him out.

"So, like I said, you're gonna want to write to the

National Personnel Records Center. They deal with all the military records. They got this form. Takes, like, six weeks."

Daniel took her hand like an ardent suitor. "What's your name?"

"Debbie."

"Debbie. I need to find this man right now. *Today*. It's *life and death*." He looked earnestly into her eyes. "Do you understand me? Debbie?"

She may have been a bureaucrat by training, but she could feel her heart melting under his intense gaze. "Harry ... what? Who did you say you're looking for?"

"Finley. Harry Finley."

"1939. That'd make him pretty damn old, huh?" She giggled girlishly.

Daniel couldn't afford to lose his new-won ally, so he giggled right along with her.

"All right," she continued. "See, I got this friend. Works at this locator service in San Antonio. Lemme see what he can do. Might take a coupla days. They get pretty busy." She scribbled some numbers on a piece of paper. "Call me after twelve. That's when I come in. If Susan answers, ask for me, *Debbie*." She gave him a slow smile. "Gave you my home number too." She shot him a little wink. "Just in case."

CHAPTER FOURTEEN

Felix and Nat had decided that Daniel had followed them home and they were going to keep him. But, of course, they had to hide him from adults, who tended to be unreasonable when eleven-year-old boys wanted to do something out of the ordinary, like bungee jump, drive a car, drink coffee or adopt an airman recently released from a state of cryogenic suspension.

Also Daniel, Felix and Nat had agreed that they couldn't be seen together all that much for fear of arousing suspicion. Besides, the two boys had an appointment later that evening that they couldn't afford to miss.

Nat raided his house and stuffed his backpack full of provisions that he smuggled out to the treehouse, which was the obvious place to hide out.

Daniel was still in a daze from the information in the newspaper. He hardly reacted when Felix and Nat started unpacking the loot.

Nat pulled a flashlight out of the backpack. "Like I said, you can stay more than one night if you need to. I made some sandwiches. Peanut butter, jelly and banana, okay?"

"Yeah," said Daniel, "just what I wanted."

"I *told* you he'd like them," said Felix triumphantly.

"Okay. You got your dinner." Nat pulled a six-pack of fruit juice out of the pack. "Drink. And dessert – Twinkies. And this." The last item was the most interesting – a giant history book, *Chronicles of America*. "Thought you might want to catch up some more. On history and stuff."

"It's mine," said Felix. "My dad got it for my eleventh birthday."

A car horn sounded in the street in front of the house. "Uh-uh," said Nat. "That's for us."

Daniel was looking at the fruit-juice boxes. "How do these work?"

"Oh. Here, let me show you." Nat stripped the plastic straw off the side of the box and speared it through the hole. "You push the straw in like this."

"Oh, thanks."

"No sweat."

Claire, Nat's mother, had come to the back door of the house.

"Nat! Felix!"

Daniel peered through the cracks between the wooden planks of the treehouse wall.

"Mrs Watson is here!"

"Gotta go," said Felix.

"Hey, we'd hang out, but there's this Boy Scout camp orientation meeting thing we're not allowed to miss. But we'll drop in and say hi when we get back. Okay?"

"Okay."

"Do you like my treehouse?"

"Yeah," said Daniel. "It's swell."

Nat's thin chest swelled with pride. "Cool. Okay. See ya later."

Once Nat and Felix were gone, Daniel sipped some juice and hunkered down with the history book. For the next two hours he found himself in a state of absolute amazement. So much had happened. So much good and bad had taken place in half a century. When he had gone under, the United States of America had possessed a military machine the same size as the Greek army; now it was the greatest military power in the history of the world.

Daniel turned the pages, staring at the pictures, illustrations of what the book called "The American Century". *And I have missed fifty whole years of it*, he thought ruefully.

He read about World War II, the Nazi death camps and the ferocious war against Japan in the Far East, the atomic bomb, the United Nations, Marilyn Monroe, Elvis Presley, the assassination of a President. He had to stop from time to time to shake his head, as if to clear it or risk information overload.

But the greatest shock came late in the day. Flipping through the book, he stopped at a set of illustrations, and one image leaped up off the page at him. It was a photograph he had seen before: the photograph Helen had taken of the striking mill worker and his children back in 1939. Stunned, he slumped back against the wall of the treehouse, the book slipping out of his lap.

He wasn't sure how long he sat like that, too dazed and shocked to do anything, but a sound brought him to his senses – or at least close to them.

A car had drawn up next to the house, and a man emerged, a big man, staggering slightly as if he'd had a drink or two too many. Nat had not mentioned his father, and Daniel couldn't help but wonder if this rather unpleasant-looking guy was part of the family.

If he was Nat's father, he was not welcome. It was plain from the look on Claire's face that she was not happy to see him – she even tried to block his entry into the house, but he pushed by her.

Daniel was riveted by the scene unfolding in the house. It was hard to see exactly what was going on, but he could hear clearly the sounds of a spirited argument. Inside the house something shattered, and Claire shrieked. There followed the ugly noise of a fist hitting flesh.

That was all Daniel needed. He jumped from the treehouse, sprinted across the lawn and went barreling in through the back door of the house.

The man had Claire down on the floor and his fist was raised to hit her hard. Daniel fell on him like an attack dog, grabbing a handful of black hair, yanking him off the woman. Then he punched him hard in the face, knocking him to the floor.

"Say, why don't you get up? And then get out," ordered Daniel.

"Who are you?" demanded the man.

"Good question," said Claire.

The man was on his feet again, throwing himself at Daniel. He was big, but he was slow, and Daniel had no problem spearing him in the belly with his elbow, then he punched him in the face once, twice, then over and over again. He was propeling the man toward the front door of the house with his fists.

Daniel threw open the door. "Out," he said, booting the man into the night. He turned to Claire. "Sorry about that."

Claire was staring at him, transfixed, like a deer caught in the twin beams of bright headlights.

"Who . . .?"

"I uh, was walking past. Past your house. I heard you scream."

Claire buried her face in her hands, upset, angry, embarrassed all at once. She sobbed a little, then almost immediately tried to pull herself together.

"God," she moaned, "I'm shaking."

Daniel helped her down on to the couch. "You're okay. You look okay."

She was still numb. She perched on the edge of the couch trying to comprehend all that had happened in the last ten minutes.

"You sure you're okay?"

Claire nodded.

Daniel stooped and picked up a twenty-dollar bill that was on the floor. He didn't know much about Nat and Claire, but he had figured out that they were not so rich that they left money lying about like that.

"Must have been his," he said. "I'm sure he'd want you to have it." He thrust the money into her trembling hands.

She stirred herself when she noticed his raw and torn knuckles. "You're bleeding."

"Oh. Heck, bleeding's nothing. Bleeding stops. I'm fine. Don't worry about it."

Claire was on her feet, walking briskly down the hall as if she needed a crisis of her own to take control of. "I can clean it up real quick."

Daniel flicked his hand as though trying to wave the pain out of it. "Really, this is barely anything. It's a scratch, that's all."

Claire returned to the living room carrying a first-aid kit. She sat down on the couch and patted the spot next to her, inviting Daniel to join her.

"It's no scratch. It's a gash. I'm a nurse, and I know gashes when I see 'em. Sit down."

Daniel sat down reluctantly. He didn't like any fussing about health or well-being. "Please, it's nothing."

"It's the least I can do. You might just have saved my life there."

"Naw . . ."

"Well, maybe." She opened the kit and poked around inside. She pulled out some balls of cotton and a bottle of disinfectant.

"This'll sting," she said, dabbing at his bloody knuckles.

If it stung, Daniel didn't show it. He gazed at her, and she could feel the questions in his look.

"That guy," she grumbled. "That was Fred. I've known some real assholes in my life, but that guy . . . He could give lessons."

Now it was Daniel's turn to look surprised. He was scarcely able to believe the word he had heard on her lips. Women – nice women, mothers, nurses – didn't talk like that in 1939.

"Fred's a drunk," she continued. "Which, by the way, is the least of his problems."

"It is?"

"Yeah. He's got no spine. No decency. He's a prick, and I knew it the day I met him."

"He's a what?"

"Prick." She smiled at him. "Oh, I know what you're thinking, but I haven't gone out with him in two years. Maybe even longer. But every once in a while he comes back. Like those storms over in Japan, you know? The violent ones that destroy the villages? *That's Fred.* What did you say your name is?"

"Daniel."

"Oh," she said brightly. "I knew a Danny once. He was worse than Fred." She thought about it for a moment. "Well, maybe not that bad."

She took out some bandage tape and swathed his knuckles. "So, Daniel, what do you do? Besides look for signs of domestic trouble, that is?"

"I'm an Air Corps lieutenant. I test airplanes."

"Oh, yeah? And when you're off duty you go around saving lives?"

Daniel smiled. "I guess so. It's not really full-time work."

Claire was looking into his eyes. "You should hang around here. Me and Nat – Nat's my son – we need saving about three times a week." She laughed. "I'm Claire. In case you were a little curious."

His hand was already in hers, but they shook anyway. "How do you do?"

From outside came the sound of a car drawing up. Claire and Daniel looked at each other, then to the window.

"You don't think Fred might pay us another visit do you?" she asked apprehensively.

"No, I doubt it."

A moment later Felix and Nat entered. Each was carrying various bits and pieces of Boy Scout equipment – a canteen, a compass, a whistle, a Scout knife and a copy of the Boy Scout manual. Both boys had their heads down, puzzling over the handbook.

"A scout never shirks nor grumbles at hardships," Felix read aloud. "So what the hell are shirks?"

"Hi, guys," said Claire.

"Hmmm, shirks . . ." Nat mulled it over. "Hi, Mom," he added as an afterthought.

"We have company."

Both boys looked up, and both of them immediately dropped all their newly acquired gear.

"Come here, I want you to meet someone. This is my son Nat and that's his friend Felix. This is Daniel."

Both kids stood stock-still, their eyes bulging out of their heads.

"Guys?" said Daniel. "You okay?"

"Hi," said Felix.

"Hi," said Nat.

"Hey, guess what?" said Claire. "Daniel's a pilot."

"Wow," said Nat without much enthusiasm. "You're kidding."

Claire nudged her son. "I see you found your jacket. Still think you saw a frozen guy?"

Nat did his best to force a laugh. "Gee, I guess not."

"Good. I'm going to see what I can burn for dinner," said Claire, retreating into the kitchen.

Felix and Nat pounced on Daniel. "*What happened?*" they demanded.

"What happened? Some jerk showed up, and I helped your Mom get rid of him. That's what happened. Now it's time to leave. Time to get out of here."

Nat grabbed him by the arm. "Wait – the couch is okay. Or you can have my room – I got a glow-in-the-dark universe on the ceiling."

Daniel put his hand on Nat's shoulder gently. "Nat, I'm a *stranger*. Your mother is not going to let a stranger sleep in her house."

"Wanna bet?"

Right after dinner – which was as badly incinerated as usual but which Daniel consumed without raising an eyebrow – Claire asked him where he was living. This called for much hemming and hawing on Daniel's part, but he did finally let slip that he had just arrived in town and had not yet arranged a place to stay. That was all it took . . .

Claire made up the living-room couch, Daniel helping to fold the sheets over the cushions. She chattered away, telling him about the idiosyncrasies of the house.

"The toothpaste is in the mirror cabinet, and there's a new toothbrush there too. Towels are below the sink. And if you want hot water, turn the faucet to four o'clock, then when it's warm, turn it to eleven, then back to nine. It's sort of like cracking a safe."

"Claire, this is awfully nice of you. You don't know the first thing about me."

"Well, I figure if you were gonna kill me, you would have let Fred do it. Anyway, you've got an honest smile."

The living room was, of course, home to the family television, and Daniel watched every minute of programing between dinner and bedtime. He never took his eyes off the screen, not even during commercials. He was dazzled, amazed, that a small brown box could transport him from a bar in Boston populated by very funny make-believe people to a famine in Africa that was actually happening right at that minute as they sat watching in a comfortable living room.

Claire and Nat seemed completely blasé about this captivating invention. How, Daniel wondered, could they keep reality and illusion separate?

"Well," said Nat, when Claire was out of the room. "It's called television."

"Yeah, I saw it at the World's Fair. They called it the modern miracle of communication. That was in the summer of 1939. In New York."

Nat shrugged. "Well, today it's no big deal. And, basically, people just watch it when they have nothing better to do. They say kids watch too much TV as it is. But, you know, the thrill kinda wears off after a while."

Daniel was still transfixed. "I think it's astounding. It's like having a movie theater in your own home."

"No. That's what a VCR is for."

"A what?"

"A video-cassette recorder. It plays movies in your home. Through your TV set," said Nat.

"You're kidding, right?"

"No, really. Lots of people – most people – have one. We don't. I asked my Mom for one, and she said maybe we'll get one at Christmastime."

Daniel turned back to the television, gazing at it with wonder in his eyes.

Nat watched him for a moment. "Felix and I need to get our Boy Scout uniforms. My Mom's too busy to take us. Wanna take us some time? She won't mind."

But Daniel could not take his eyes off the set. He was devouring the weather report on the evening news. "No."

"Oh." Nat looked a little disappointed, but Daniel didn't notice.

"Goodnight," he said.

Daniel hardly heard him.

CHAPTER FIFTEEN

Daniel watched TV until he could no longer keep his eyes open. Somewhere deep in the wastelands of pre-dawn television he fell asleep, visions of the Home Shopping Network dancing in his head. It took him a moment or two to remember where he was when Nat nudged him awake the next morning.

"Daniel! Get up!"

Daniel opened his eyes a crack and stared at the small boy, trying to remember who this little fellow was.

"Huh?"

"That guy called back! Said he knows Harry Finley. He lives in the next town over. Packardville. It's about an hour from here. Here's the address." Nat thrust a scrap of paper into Daniel's hand.

"Harry?" Then it all came back to him in a rush – the kaleidoscopic events of the previous day and the sickening predicament he was now in. The piece of paper that Nat had given him had the effect of a jolt of caffeine coursing through his system. Daniel bounded out of bed and immediately started pulling on his blue jeans.

"I gotta get going!"

Nat looked a little panicky. "Wait! Wait! Before you go, we're going to Wings of Freedom, right? You know what that is, don't you? Wings of Freedom? The air show? You can see your friend after."

"What's all the commotion about?" Claire walked

in, combing her hair. She looked fresh and well rested, put back together after the turbulence of the evening before. She seemed genuinely pleased to see Daniel that morning.

"I want Daniel to come to the Wings of Freedom air show."

"I'd love to, but I can't, Nat."

Claire started to strip the sheets off the couch. "So how was it? The couch. Were you okay?"

"Very comfortable, thank you," said Daniel with a smile. "Let me help you with those."

"I got it."

"Claire, you're one of the kindest people I ever met."

Claire began to fold the sheets briskly. "Well, you haven't seen my temper."

"Yeah," Nat agreed. "You haven't seen *that*."

"How about some breakfast?" asked Claire.

Daniel was anxious to get going. "Thanks, I'd love to, but I have to meet an old friend."

"You sure? Don't let that lousy dinner put you off. Breakfast is a whole different matter. I'm a hell of a good defroster."

"Defroster?" It struck Daniel that a talent for defrosting seemed to run in the family. "I'm sorry, I can't. I have to go. I'm already late." He didn't add what he was thinking: *About fifty years late.*

Nat was so anxious that he was jumping up and down like a puppy. The chance to go to an air show with a real live pilot was too good an opportunity to pass up.

"Wait, Daniel. Come to the air show. It's so cool. There are all kinds of planes. Old ones, new ones. Stunts. Stuff like that."

"Nat, he said he's busy. Besides, he deals with planes all the time. Every day. Jets are old news to our friend here."

For a moment Nat teetered on the edge of telling his mother exactly how much Daniel actually knew about jets, but he managed to keep silent.

"Old hat," agreed Daniel. "I have to go now. Thanks. Thank you." He proffered his bandaged hand. "I don't know how to thank you for your kindness."

"It was nothing at all."

"Good luck," said Daniel, heading for the door.

Nat and Claire watched him walk out of the house.

"Well," she said. "Kind of a strange guy. Nice, but definitely strange. There's more going on with him than he wanted to let on about." She turned back to folding the sheets. "I guess that's that."

Nat looked at his mother. She would never know the half of it.

It took a lot longer than an hour for Daniel to get to Packardville. He started walking, his thumb stuck out, expecting to get a ride in a matter of minutes. But car after car roared by him, the drivers not giving him so much as a glance. Daniel couldn't understand it. The cars were almost all empty of passengers, and in Daniel's day people were always picking up hitch-hikers to have someone to talk to, to help pass the time on the drive.

"Times change," he mumbled aloud as he trudged along. He ended up walking all the way and was dusty and footsore by the time he found the address on the piece of paper.

Harry lived in a pretty select part of the town. The

neighborhood was quiet. The streets were shady and tree-lined, the houses large and imposing, set back from the road and surrounded by lush gardens. Through hedges and the cracks in tall fences Daniel could make out dun-colored tennis courts and the cool blue of swimming pools.

Daniel whistled low. "Harry did pretty well for himself," he said when he found the Finley residence. It was a large, red-brick house with tall, elegant white pillars adorning the façade.

Daniel ran up the steps, pressed the doorbell and heard quiet chimes ring deep within the house. He was happy and relieved that his ordeal was almost over, but he was jittery too, nervous about confronting a piece of his long-ago past. His mind spun with questions he couldn't wait to ask.

Presently the door was opened by a woman in a black maid's uniform. For a moment Daniel was taken aback. Maids weren't exactly Harry's and Blanche's style – at least they hadn't been half a century earlier. Daniel hoped that his old friend hadn't gone all high-and-mighty on him. It seemed unlikely, but if a machine could be invented that answered telephones, then it was conceivable that Harry could have turned into a snob.

"Yes?" said the house keeper.

"I'm here to see Harry Finley."

She nodded. "Please come in."

The house keeper led him into the house and parked him in a richly appointed study. There were books in tall carved book cases, a huge desk and bits of antique bric-à-brac scattered here and there. The room didn't look like anything Harry and Blanche would have liked, but Daniel figured things were different when you were rich. He was afraid to touch anything, and he felt his jitters increase in intensity. Nervously he wiped his palms on his pants.

Then the study door opened, and a portly, well-dressed man entered the room. He had a prominent nose and swept-back white hair. The man smiled pleasantly enough, but his eyes betrayed no recognition. "And what can I do for you, young man?"

Daniel half closed his eyes, trying to see Harry Finley, *his* Harry Finley, in the old man's face. It was like comparing two photographs: the "before" was the one Daniel carried in his mind. The "after" was the elderly fellow who stood before him now.

"May I help you?" he repeated.

"You are . . . Harry? Harry Finley?"

"That's right."

Daniel couldn't see it. "You?"

The old man looked puzzled. "Yes. I'm Harry Finley. What can I do for you?"

Daniel shook his head. "Do you know me?"

"No."

"Oh."

Harry Finley looked baffled. "Are you all right?"

Daniel felt a great cold wave of disappointment washing over him. "I'm . . . I'm sorry. You're not the . . . Do you know another Harry Finley? Do you know a Harry Finley who is a scientist?"

"No, sir, I don't. I have only met one other Harry Finley in my entire life."

"You *did*? Where?"

"Baltimore. It was years ago. But he wasn't a scientist either. As I recall it, he was in the wholesale upholstery business."

Daniel's shoulders slumped, and he shook his head slowly, dejection showing Clearly on his face. "Damn."

Harry Finley smiled kindly, sad that he had plainly caused this stranger pain. "Sorry to disappoint you."

"It's not your fault," said Daniel turning for the door.

Daniel trudged slowly down the street, quite unaware of where he was going. His mind was spinning out of control, wild with his crazy dilemma, a quandary he could see no way out of. He tried to urge himself to think. There was no one he could tell his story to, no one he could trust.

Any authority he confided in – like Captain Wilcox – would think he was crazy and arrange a one-way trip to the nearest nut house. The only people who really knew what happened, who really understood, were two eleven-year-old boys . . .

"Oh, brother," Daniel sighed. "You've really done it this time."

Then he seemed to wake up, as if he had been in a deep sleep. He found himself standing at the side of a freeway, a great rushing torrent of traffic six lanes across. Cars and trucks were racing past him in both directions, oblivious to him. Like a man on the bank of an uncrossable river, Daniel could only stare at the cars, helpless and lost. He was so low, so powerless, so suffused with sadness, that all he wanted to do was lie down and die, right there by the noisy, smoky stream of traffic.

Something in the sky caught his eye. It seemed to come like a sign from heaven. It was far away, but with a practiced pilot's eye he recognized the aircraft's silhouette instantly. It was a B-25, flying straight and true toward him, both engines thundering. It passed overhead, the engine noise drowning out the traffic for a moment.

"Wow!" Daniel yelled. "What a beauty!"

Then he started in the direction the airplane had gone, down the bank along the highway. Soon he was running as fast as he could, as if he were trying to catch the silver tail of his old aircraft.

The Wings of Freedom air show, held at the local airport, was like a county fair but with airplanes instead of prize livestock, flower shows and giant vegetables. The local high school's marching band performed, and there were booths selling hot dogs and soft drinks, cotton candy and candy apples.

The stars of the show, though, were the aircraft assembled on the runway. High over the air field two stunt planes wowed the crowd, diving and flipping, soaring through the blue sky like eagles.

There were vintage biplanes, perfectly restored. There was a World War I Spad, sporting the insignia of the famous "Hat in a Ring" 94th Aero Squadron, parked on the hardstand next to a British Bristol F-2B fighter. Next to that was a spotless American Boeing-Stearman A-73 Trainer.

There were planes that were closer in vintage to Daniel's era. The most famous American aircraft of the twenties and thirties was there too, the Boeing P-26, nicknamed the "pea shooter." It was well known for being the first all-metal aircraft and the first mono-plane ever employed by the US Army Air Corps. The sun glinted off a perfectly restored Curtiss P-36 Hawk, the plane that Daniel had learned to fly on. And the *pièce de résistance* was the B-25, sitting in the middle of the flock like a queen surrounded by her admiring courtiers.

There were lethal-looking fighters and bombers that he could not identify, products of a more recent era, machines that had been developed during Daniel's long sleep.

Daniel wished he could see the beautiful machines close up instead of peering through the cyclone fence. But the man taking tickets at the turnstile had told him that admission was five dollars. To the penniless Daniel it might as well have been a thousand.

But how he longed to see those planes! From where he stood he couldn't make out the B-25 in any detail, and he yearned to see it, like a new father peering at his baby through a maternity-ward window.

Daniel glanced quickly to left and right. There was no one around who was paying him the slightest bit of attention. Swiftly he clambered over the fence.

Nat and Felix, Claire and John were sitting in the grandstand, gazing aloft, mouths open, watching the stunt fliers. The two planes were flying upside down, zooming along wing tip to wing tip.

"How come they don't fall out?" Nat wondered aloud.

"Because they're *professionals*," Felix explained.

John took his eyes off the planes long enough to shoot a glance at Claire. "How about tomorrow night?" he asked.

Claire shaded her eyes against the bright sun. "Tomorrow night? What about it?"

"Dinner?"

"Okay," said Claire.

John smiled to himself and turned back to the planes, his heart flying now.

Feeling like a criminal, Daniel skulked among the crowd gathered around the B-25 and watched as the ground crew bustled around their baby. Daniel grinned to himself. He knew how proprietorial crews could be about their aircraft, and he was glad to see this one was well taken care of.

The B-25 was a thing of beauty. The hull was smooth and buffed to a high sheen. He touched it tenderly, caressing the silky aluminum skin, overcome like a parent who realizes that his little girl has finally grown up.

He examined the wings, tears springing into his eyes. "Wright Cyclones . . . Now *those* are classic engines."

"I'll say. They certainly knew how to make a plane back in the old days."

Daniel turned. The chief of the ground crew was wiping an oil spot from the lower flap.

"You certainly know your engines," the man said.

"Oh," said Daniel. "I'm just an amateur."

"But you know machinery when you see it. Young people don't usually pay too much attention to the old classics like this one. They're all heavy into jets. You know."

"Oh, yeah. Heavy into jets," repeated Daniel, wondering just what that might mean.

The mechanic gestured toward the open hatch in the side of the plane. "We're open to the public, so take a look inside. If you love old airplanes, you'll like what you see."

His heart pounding with anticipation, Daniel swung himself into the plane and immediately felt as if he had never been away, as if he had stepped from this plane a few hours – not a few decades – before.

Everything was just as he had left it. He made his way through the fuselage, moving past the waist gunner's position, under the dome of the top turret, through the navigator-radio post, past the bombardier's sight and into the cockpit.

Daniel settled in the pilot's seat and put his hands on the controls. It was like coming home, like settling in the beat-up old armchair he used to have in his living room. He sighed with pleasure.

Everything fit, comfortably, like a pair of old blue jeans. He noticed that this craft had been equipped with a more powerful radio than they had had and that radar, in its infancy in 1939, was prominently displayed. In the prototype he had flown the cockpit layout had not been finalized, and he felt a stab of pride in the team he had been part of so long ago. They had designed a perfect flight deck, a model that any pilot would admire.

Suddenly he longed to be back in his old life, back in those exciting days, part of the team that built this plane. Back with Helen . . .

Daniel gazed out through the canopy, over the snub prow of the nose, and sighed. In that moment he wished he could fire up those two big engines, take this plane into the sky and fly back to his past, his happy past.

CHAPTER SIXTEEN

But he couldn't.

Daniel suddenly became aware of someone watching him. He half turned in the seat and saw a man and a little boy standing behind the cockpit, patiently waiting for their turn to sit in the pilot's seat.

Daniel jumped to his feet. "I'm sorry. I guess I was sorta . . . Just day dreaming, I guess."

"That's easy to do with a view like that." The man pointed up through the canopy into the deep-blue sky.

"Yeah," Daniel said, pushing by them.

He heard the little boy whisper, "I thought he'd never get out of there."

Deep in his soul he felt a stab of intense pain as he made his way out of the aircraft. It had struck him hard, this sudden and intense realization that the great project of his youth was now an antique, a thing of the past to be gawked at by tourists – and that he was one of them.

The "old days" the ground crewman had said. Daniel was from the "old days." They were his time, his *present* – now the distant past. And he was just as much a relic as this grand old B-25.

"Harry," he whispered. "Where are you?"

Daniel wandered blindly through the crowd, not noticing anything except the clock on the wall of a refreshment stand. It was after twelve and time to check in with Debbie. Maybe she had found Harry for him – maybe he was just a phone call away from finding Harry. Except he didn't even have the money to make a phone call.

For a moment he despaired, discouraged by the immensity of the problems he had to surmount. "Damn," he groaned.

But he couldn't give up. He was an officer in the United States Army Air Corps, and he had been trained to think on his feet. He was determined to do just that.

On the far side of the fairground was an information and first-aid booth, which doubled as a depository for objects lost and found. It also had a telephone.

Daniel noticed that one of the objects that had been lost but not yet found was a six-year-old boy, who stood wailing and bawling his eyes out in a corner while one of the volunteers tried to distract him with an impressive array of junk food.

"Poor little fellow," said Daniel. "Is he lost?"

"Yes," said the harried-looking woman who had the task of taking care of the little boy. "He's not yours, by any chance, is he?"

"'Fraid not. But, you know, he looks kind of familiar."

"He does?" Hope suddenly burned bright in her eyes.

"Yeah. He looks like a kid who lives in my neighborhood."

"He does? What's his name? I can't get him to tell me."

Daniel laughed. "I don't know. He's just one of the neighborhood kids."

"Oh," said the volunteer, dejectedly.

"But my wife might know."

"She might?" The woman perked up again.

"If I could just give her a call . . ."

"Oh, would you, please?"

Daniel grabbed the phone and dialed Debbie's number quickly, hunching over the phone, praying that the child's loud crying would drown out his words.

"I was hoping maybe you heard something," he said quickly. "No? Do you think there's any way you could rush it? It's just that –" Daniel sighed in frustration. "Sure, I'll try later." *If I can ever get to use a phone again*, he added mentally. Furious, he slammed down the phone. "Damn!"

The woman looked up from the kid.

"Uh, sorry," mumbled Daniel. "I'm afraid that I was mistaken. That's not the same little boy. Sorry."

Daniel shuffled out of the booth, the woman staring after him curiously. He stumbled through the crowd, walking like a crazy man. People saw him coming and got out of his way. He lumbered into a trash can, tipping it over, but he was unaware of it. Despair was weighing down on him even more heavily than before. It felt like it was crushing him. Slowly he sank down on to one of the grandstand benches and put his head in his hands.

Daniel was aware of someone standing close, and out of the hubbub of the crowd and the din of aircraft he heard a voice.

"Would you quit following me? Okay?"

He looked up, startled, and saw Claire smiling down at him. She held a cardboard tray laden with Cokes and hot dogs. Behind her a P-51 Mustang tore into the sky.

"What's the matter?" she asked. "Can't find anyone to rescue?" She lowered the tray. "Want a hot dog?"

"No, thanks."

Claire sat down next to him. "I've been told I listen exceptionally well. If you want to tell me anything, that is."

Daniel sighed heavily and shook his head, trying to gather his thoughts and put them into words. "Did you ever . . . ? Have you ever felt . . . lost?"

Claire grinned. "Hey, I invented that. That's mine. Wrote the book."

"I don't know what I'm supposed to do. My buddy was supposed to be here when I woke up. Today. He used to live in town. And I can't find him now." He paused for a moment and studied her face intently. "I know this sounds melodramatic, but he's all I have left."

"And, what, you thought maybe he was in that trash can you knocked over?"

Daniel looked at her uncomprehendingly. "Trash can? What trash can?"

"You knocked over a trash can."

"I did?"

"I'm sorry I said that. I'm sorry. That was . . . I'm sorry. You could always go back home, right?"

Their eyes met and locked for a long time.

"I lost someone very close to me," said Daniel softly.

"Oh." Claire could feel the sorrow emanating from him like heat.

"That's why I left," he continued. "That's why I don't have any money or clothes or a place to stay. I just left. Where I was going to end up was the last thing on my mind."

Claire nodded. "Hey, you know, I did that once. I just upped and ran away. It was a different situation, but it's true, what you said." She shrugged. "You don't think about where you're going – you just go."

Neither of them noticed John approaching. He threaded his way through the crowd and saw Claire sitting with a handsome stranger. He worked hard to suppress the sharp twinge of jealousy that struck him.

"Everything okay?"

Claire jumped to her feet. "Sure. Hey, John, this is Daniel. Daniel, meet John."

The two men shook hands.

"Daniel is going to be staying with us for a few days until he finds a friend of his."

"I am?" said Daniel, startled.

John looked inquiringly at Claire. "He is?"

"It's okay. He's gonna take the kids to get their Boy Scout uniforms."

"I am?"

"He is?"

"Yep," said Claire.

Miraculously, John managed a smile. "Well, it's good to know you, Daniel. Good to know you."

The adults and Nat and Felix spent the rest of the afternoon at the air show, Daniel managing to forget his troubles for a while, losing himself in the arcana of the aircraft at the show. He entranced the kids with his knowledge of airplanes and airplane lore, a display of erudition that plunged John into depression. If the battle for Claire's heart could be won by winning over her son, then this stranger was streaking into the lead.

By the time they got home that night all of Daniel's

discouragement had returned, wrapping around him like a cold shroud. His only hope now was that Debbie had found some trace of Harry.

He waited until Claire and Nat were in the kitchen, then he picked up the phone and dialed Debbie's home number, hoping desperately that she had found out something, anything, that might be able to help him.

But not only did he not get any information about Harry – he couldn't even get Debbie on the phone. Instead he got that amazing invention, her answering machine.

Daniel felt a little silly talking to a machine. "Uh ... Hi, machine. Uh, anyway, it's Daniel again. I'm staying at ... 992-4342. So if you hear anything, please call me here. Thanks, Debbie. Uh ... 'bye, machine."

Daniel placed the phone on its cradle. Then his hand started to shake uncontrollably, his grip tightening involuntarily on the receiver. His whole arm trembled for a moment, then gradually the sensation died away.

CHAPTER SEVENTEEN

Boy Scout camp was fast approaching, and the equipment and uniform store was a scarcely contained riot of kids, harried shop clerks and hot-and-bothered parents. Daniel delivered Nat and Felix into the hands of one of the salesmen and settled in a chair in a corner, hoping to stay out of the maelstrom.

He was out of luck. A moment after he sat down a little boy ran by, neatly spilling half a cup of Coca-Cola in his lap.

Daniel jumped to his feet, wiping at his blue jeans. "Aw, no. Gee."

The kid stopped and stared at him, working out in his mind just who was to blame for this mishap – Daniel for sitting where he was sitting or himself for being careless. Reluctantly he decided that the blame was his.

"Sorry, sir. I'm really sorry."

"Yeah. Don't worry about it."

"Okay." The kid hurried away, escaping the scene of the crime.

Just then Nat and Felix emerged from the dressing room wearing their Boy Scout uniforms, wide smiles on their faces. The skinny chests of both boys were puffed out with pride, like soldiers about to receive the Congressional Medal of Honor. Both stood at attention in front of Daniel.

"So?" asked Nat. "How do we look?"

"Be honest," cautioned Felix.

"Yeah," agreed Nat. "We want your honest opinion."

"Uh, not bad," said Daniel without enthusiasm.

Nat looked puzzled. "Not bad? Is that supposed to mean that we look good?"

Daniel shrugged. "Sure, yeah."

"So how come you don't say we look good?" asked Felix.

"You look good, okay? Can we get out of this place now?"

"We *do*?"

Felix and Nat beamed at each other. "Wow," said Nat. "We look good. Really?"

"Told you we looked good," said Felix happily.

Nat looked back to Daniel. "Would you say that we look *bitchin'*?"

"Bitchin'? No. I just told you that you look good. Not bitchin'."

Nat shook his head quickly. "You don't understand. Nowadays, bitchin' *is* good."

"Oh. In that case, yeah, you look bitchin'."

Nat and Felix slapped high fives at each other. "*We look bitchin'.*"

Felix went to his house to drop off his Scout uniform, and Nat and Daniel went straight to the answering machine when they got home. Nat examined the device and shook his head.

"Anything?" asked Daniel hopefully.

Nat shook his head slowly. "Nope."

"How can you tell? You can tell just by looking at it?"

"Yup. See?" He pointed at the machine. "The red light isn't blinking, so that means that no one called."

The frustration on Daniel's face was obvious. He slapped a fist into the palm of his hand. "Dang."

"Now what are you going to do?" asked Nat.

Daniel thought for a moment. "What do you want for dinner?" he asked.

"Dinner?" said Nat. "You're making dinner?"

Daniel shrugged. "Gotta do something."

Nat trailed Daniel into the kitchen and watched while he inspected the cupboards for provisions. He pulled out a few cans and some spices and then investigated the contents of the refrigerator.

"Hey, listen," said Nat.

Daniel took out the makings of a salad and put them on the kitchen counter. "Yeah?"

"I was thinking that maybe tomorrow . . . if you don't find your friend . . . maybe you could teach me to fly."

Daniel considered this suggestion. "Might be tough," he said after a while.

"How come?"

"Well, first off, I don't have a flight jacket. Secondly, I don't have an airplane."

"Oh."

Daniel busied himself with the vegetables, tearing up lettuce and rinsing it under the faucet.

After a long silence Nat spoke. "My father left when I was one."

"He did?"

Nat nodded. "Just thought you might want to know that."

"I don't think it's really any of my business."

"He left when I was one, and he hasn't talked to us since."

"Thanks." Daniel knew a building case of the guilts

when he heard one. It wasn't that he didn't want to teach Nat how to fly. It was just that he couldn't. It really did require the services of an airplane. And, besides, he had other, more pressing, things on his mind just at the moment.

Nat sighed. "Can I help you out?"

"You could find Harry Finley," said Daniel wistfully.

"I meant, can I help you with dinner?"

"Oh, yeah, I guess so." Daniel nodded and handed him an onion. "Here, dice this."

Nat beamed. "Cool."

Peeling the onion wasn't easy, and neither was dicing it. Nat did not stand much higher than the counter top, so it didn't take long for him to get a very bad case of onion tears. But he struggled on manfully.

"Do you think it would be okay for me to invite Felix over for dinner? Usually when he eats here my mother cooks, and you know she's not the greatest cook in the world."

"How do you know I'll be any better?"

"You gotta be." Nat sniffed and snuffled noisily.

Daniel stopped what he was doing and looked at the boy as if seeing him for the first time.

Here was this poor kid, the child of a single parent. He had never known his father. He had one friend in the whole world. Daniel had the feeling that Felix and Nat were the outcasts of their junior high school class, boys who didn't run with the cool kids and who were sticking together for mutual aid and security. In a funny way Nat was just as much at sea in this world, just as lost, as Daniel himself.

*

Dinner – roast chicken, baked potatoes, peas and a salad – was delicious. Claire was the first to admit that. She was seated at the table, in a pair of old gray sweats, devouring the meal. Neither Felix nor Nat could remember a time when she ate so heartily or seemed so happy, so animated.

It was pouring rain outside, and every time the thunder rumbled she shivered deliciously. "Boy," she said. "It's great to be inside, all cozy like this, having a great dinner."

"Glad you like it," said Daniel.

"Like it? I *love* it." She helped herself to some more eagerly. "Guess what happened at work?"

"What?" asked Nat.

"Well, a couple of weeks ago, in the emergency room, we get a code one. That means: trauma team stand by to meet accident victims. There was a huge car wreck out on Route Five."

She speared another potato.

"Yeah?" said Daniel. "So what happened?"

"They bring in a guy. He is covered in blood. *Covered.* His heart has stopped – no time for procedure, right? They just crack his chest, and I have to massage his heart. I mean, *I actually have to hold his heart in my hands and pump it for him.* Can you believe it?"

Claire did not notice that Nat, Felix and Daniel had stopped eating at the words "crack his chest."

Claire continued, unaware of the effect her words were having on her audience. "Anyway, the guy, the guy whose heart I'm pumping, all of a sudden, *he opens his eyes.*" She put a chunk of chicken in her mouth and chewed vigorously.

"And he looks at his heart and then he looks at me and he says, 'You're holding my heart.' Can you believe that?"

The three of them could believe it, and it was plain from the looks on their faces that they had a very clear picture of the gory scene in their minds.

"'Yes, I am.' That's what I said. The anesthesiologist almost passed out." Claire chuckled. "Anyway, that was two weeks ago. Today I get to work, and guess what?"

"What?" asked Daniel.

"The guy has sent me a box of candy! A heart-shaped box of candy. Isn't that a great story?"

"Great," they all agreed, though the story had robbed them of their appetites.

"Daniel," Claire said, "this meal is fabulous."

"Thanks."

"Guys, I mean it, my taste buds are freaking out. I can't believe how good this is."

Daniel shrugged. "It's the easiest thing in the world. It's a snap."

Claire was not convinced. "Good cooks always say that. But I know from experience that if it tastes this good, it's not that easy."

The doorbell rang, and Nat was out of his seat fast, as if the bell was a starter's gun. "Mine!" he shouted. "I'll get it."

Claire turned back to her meal. "The really scary thing is that I had all this somewhere in my own cupboard. Lurking there."

"It was nothing."

"Okay. It was nothing. But taking the kids to get their uniforms: now, that was *something*. That was above and beyond the –" She stopped speaking, her fork half way to her mouth.

Nat was leading John into the kitchen. The doctor was dressed up, all decked out in a white shirt and tie, and he was wearing his best dark suit.

"Oh," he said, taking in the homey scene before him. His cheeks burned bright red.

"We have a date," said Claire, remembering his invitation of the night before.

"Am I early?" asked John.

Claire did her best to recover gracefully. "No. Not early. I'm just running a little late. Just tasting Daniel's cooking."

She daintily nibbled a bit of chicken on her fork and let it drop to her plate. "It's very good, Daniel. Very good." She stood up. "Okay. I have to go get ready. Won't be a minute."

John wasn't taken in by this charade for a moment. He settled in her vacant seat and did his best to smile.

"Hi, boys."

"Hi," said Nat and Felix in unison.

John sighed uneasily. "I'm glad I didn't bring flowers. They'd somehow increase the fool factor."

Daniel shook his head emphatically. "Oh, no, Claire was just talking about your date. Right before you got here. Wasn't she?" He appealed to Nat and Felix.

The boys nodded dutifully.

"Yep," said Nat.

"She sure was," said Felix.

John believed Daniel and the two boys just about as much as he had believed Claire's little performance a few seconds before. That is, not much.

An uncomfortable silence settled on the table. Nat

and Felix had as yet to go on a date, but they knew in their bones that forgetting about one was definitely a very serious social *faux pas*.

"So," said Daniel, "you're a doctor."

"Yes. Yes. That's right. And you're a pilot."

"That's right."

Nat and Felix watched this awkward exchange, turning from one man to the other, like spectators at a tennis match.

"Doctor . . . pilot," said John.

Daniel did his best to force a laugh. "Doctor . . . pilot," he repeated, feeling like a moron. He felt sweat at his collar and thought that if this conversation lasted much longer, he would scream. Luckily Claire saved them.

From upstairs they heard a yell. "Nat! Bring the big spaghetti pot! Now!"

The same thought raced through four minds at the same time. Why would she need a large piece of cookware to get ready to go on a date?

"*Shit!*" shouted Claire.

The two men and the two boys ran to her bedroom. Claire, wearing only a skirt, a bra and an extremely angry look, was standing in front of her closet, frantically pulling clothes out of it and throwing them on the bed.

"Are you okay?" asked Daniel, trying to see what was going on and avert his eyes at the same time – no easy task.

"Yeah," she growled. "I'm fine, except for this waterfall in my closet!" She quickly slipped on a blouse and buttoned it. Everyone felt better about that. "Nat, would you go and get the spaghetti pot?"

Daniel inspected the inside of the closet. Water was trickling down the wood panels from a seam in the ceiling.

"It's just a hole in the ceiling," said Daniel.

"*Just*," snapped Claire.

"Claire," said John, "we can make this another night if you want. You've got your hands full."

"No, John, I'll be right there. Really."

"If you're sure."

Claire flashed him her sweetest smile. "No, really, it's fine."

Daniel hauled a basket full of sodden underwear from the closet and handed it to her. "I can fix this. Got any tools? Hammer, nails, roofing paper, shingles?"

"I got the hammer part," said Claire.

"It's a start."

"Can I help at all?" asked John.

Nat lugged the big aluminum spaghetti pot into the bedroom and handed it to Daniel. He positioned it under the leak.

"Is . . . is there still a hardware store?" asked Daniel uncertainly.

"What kind of question is that?" said Claire. "*Of course* there's still a hardware store."

Daniel looked relieved. "I'll get what I need and fix it tomorrow. Don't worry. Go to dinner."

Claire beamed. "Really?"

"Just have fun," said Daniel.

Claire tucked in her blouse and slipped on her shoes. Then she paused to check her hair in the mirror on the dresser. She caught sight of the twenty-dollar bill she had left there.

"Here," she said, giving the money to Daniel. "The roof will be on our old friend Fred. So to speak."

Nat, Felix and Daniel saw them to the door and waved them out into the rain. Just before they closed the door they heard Claire say, "I'm starving, John. I hope you've chosen some place good."

The instant the door was shut Nat and Felix burst into peals of laughter.

Daniel smiled. "Hey, come on. It's not funny. I felt bad for the guy. Didn't you?"

CHAPTER EIGHTEEN

The giant True-Value hardware store was the most amazing place Daniel had yet encountered here in the future, a treasure house of inventions. He had filled his basket quickly with the things he needed – old-fashioned, low-tech things like nails and shingles – and he then spent an hour wandering the aisles, looking unbelievingly at the stupendous modern merchandise.

There were lawnmowers you could ride on like little tractors. There were machines for blowing – not shoveling – snow out of driveways. His mind boggled at the power tools. There were electric shears that could trim your hedges in a few seconds, belt sanders and table saws – even a gas-engined chain saw so light a child could handle it and yet powerful enough to cut down a giant California redwood.

Daniel looked in wonder at a power hammer, turning it over and over in his hands, his eyes full of wonder. "Wow!"

A sales clerk watched him curiously, then walked over and stood next to him.

"Is there something I can help you with, sir?"

"Yeah. Is this thing really what I think it is?"

"I guess so."

"You mean," Daniel said, as if he was having his leg pulled, "you mean to tell me that this shoots nails? I mean, it *hammers* for you?"

"Uh-huh," said the clerk, wondering what this lunatic was getting so excited about.

"*Automatically*? By pushing a *button*? It's an electric *hammer*?"

"That's right."

"Wow! That's brilliant! Isn't that incredible?"

The sales clerk shrugged. "Never thought about it, I guess."

"It's amazing." Daniel snatched another item from the rack. "And this is — it's an *electric screwdriver*! I don't believe it! Amazing! Just amazing!"

The sales clerk wondered if he should call security . . .

It was another hour before Daniel could drag himself out of the hardware store, but he found that there were just as many astonishing things on the street as inside.

As he waited to cross at an intersection a Chevrolet Corvette pulled up at the stop light. Daniel gasped when he saw it. It was low to the ground like a jungle cat, the side windows were blacked out, and a deep, loud bass thump blasted out of the sound system.

"That's a *car*?" Daniel shook his head, marveling at the machine.

The instant the light changed the sports car slammed into gear and sped away. Daniel watched it until it vanished around a corner.

Then, as he started to cross the street, something more astounding than the Corvette or an electric screwdriver caught his eye. Standing there on the busy main street was Jake's Diner, looking, from the outside, as if it had hardly changed at all in the last fifty years.

Daniel's jaw dropped, and he walked toward it, unable to take his eyes off the shabby old building. It might have been a mirage or a vision that would vanish the very instant he looked away.

He entered the restaurant like a pilgrim at the end of a long and difficult journey reaching a holy shrine. His eyes swam with tears as he looked around and saw that so little had changed, although there were some new appliances – a microwave oven and an electronic cash register that beeped and squeaked when the cashier tapped out a customer's check. In the corner was the phone booth . . . the last place on earth where he had known a moment of happiness.

Daniel stumbled across the room and settled in the very booth he had shared with Helen that fateful day so many years before. He was dazed to be here once again. He could see her, sense her smile, smell her perfume, hear her voice as it bubbled over with happiness about the news that *Collier's* wanted to buy her photographs.

The waitress stopped by his table, her order pad ready. "Can I help you?"

Daniel could hardly find his voice. "I . . . I'd just like to sit here a moment . . . if that's okay."

The waitress put her pencil back behind her ear. "Suit yourself," she said with a shrug.

He rubbed a hand reverently across the table top. He saw Helen knock over the salt shaker and toss a little of the salt over her left shoulder. Neither of them had known that her luck would run out just seconds afterward.

Daniel poured a few grains of salt into his palm and tossed them over his shoulder. Then he wiped a tear from his eye.

Daniel didn't know it, but at that moment, on the far side of town, someone else was discovering a piece of his past. Captain Wilcox drove on to the base and passed the warehouse slated for demolition. Acres of the junk that had been within had now been moved outside, and it was all awaiting loading on to dump trucks.

Wilcox nodded to himself. Things seemed to be going according to plan, right on schedule. Then he caught sight of the capsule, sitting forlornly on the asphalt. The captain stepped on the brake. He ran over to the object and walked around it. The nut who had appeared in his office a few days before had given a fairly detailed description of the capsule, and it certainly fit this peculiar-looking thing. But it was really too crazy to consider – wasn't it? "No," he whispered to himself. "It *can't* be . . ."

Then his stomach lurched when he realized that, indeed, it couldn't be anything else. Tied on to one of the valves was a large yellow label, a piece of paper fluttering in the breeze. With a hammering heart, Wilcox turned it over and read what was written there: "Project B (for Buford)".

CHAPTER NINETEEN

Daniel was glad he had the roof to fix. As he had said to Nat the day before, he had to do something, keep his hands busy, do *anything* to take his mind off Helen, Harry and the other ghosts of the past that haunted his tortured present.

He was up on the roof, using the hammer to lever up the old shingles. Nat and Felix were stationed at the foot of the ladder, filling him in on more of the wonders of life in the United States of America, *circa* 1992.

Naturally, the two boys had turned to one of their favorite topics of conversation, the composition and merits of various types of junk food.

"Okay, listen up," said Nat portentously. "This is important, okay?"

"Great," Daniel grumbled. "I'm learning how to be a good eleven-year-old."

"See," said Nat, like a lecturer in a classroom, "Chocodiles are just like Ding Dongs."

"But *exactly*," confirmed Felix.

"Except Chocodiles are longer," said Nat.

"Right," Felix agreed.

"Got it?"

"Got it," said Daniel.

"Now, Chocodiles and Ding Dongs are both like Ho-Hos. Almost exactly."

"Right," said Felix.

"Zingers are like Twinkies with frosting. And Suzie-Qs are kinda the same too."

"But flat."

"Yeah," said Nat. "But they're flat. And Sno Balls are a total mystery."

"Yeah. *No one* knows what's in Sno Balls."

"You see?"

Daniel was still tearing shingles out of the roof. "Perfectly."

The Dodge driven by Steven, Felix's brother, rolled to a halt at the curb in front of the house. Steven tapped the horn and leaned out the window.

"What are you doing here?" he demanded of his little brother.

"Watching."

"Watching? Watching what?"

Felix nodded toward the roof and Daniel. "Watching him."

"Well, cut it out, Quasimodo. Didn't I tell you to mow el lawno today?"

Felix put his head down and kicked the dirt at his feet. "I said I'd do it."

"*This year* would be nice."

"No problem."

"Just do it. *Now.*"

Steven wrenched his car into gear and zoomed away. Felix watched him go and sighed.

"Well, gotta go." Felix hopped on his bike. "I'll come back later."

"Okay," said Nat. When he had gone Nat turned his attention back to Daniel.

"Can I ask you something?"

"Sure."

"Remember that girl at the library?"

"Girl?"

"The girl at the library. Alice. Remember?"

"Yeah? What about her?"

"Well, she's really cool. Like, for example, she shares her lunch. Like, if she's got a brownie and someone's got an apple, she'll trade. Who does stuff like that? Plus she's really, really pretty," said Nat in a great rush of words.

"What's the question?" asked Daniel. "I didn't hear a question in there anywhere. If it was there, I missed it."

"What should I do?"

"Do? Do about what?"

"About Alice. To get her to like me. I mean, Felix says I should make her jealous. He says that's what his brother does with girls, but I don't think Alice ever even notices me, so I don't think I *could* get her jealous. D'you see?"

Daniel looked over his shoulder at the small, earnest face that was staring up at him. "Listen, you're very young. You should be thinking about other things."

"I'm eleven," said Nat stoutly. "I really like her."

Daniel hesitated a moment. "If I were you, I'd put her out of my mind. The sooner the better. Just forget about her. Trust me."

"But —"

Suddenly a swell of nausea and dizziness swept through Daniel's body. He closed his eyes, wincing at the terrible, migraine-like pain that seemed to split his skull in two.

Nat saw that he was losing his balance. "Daniel!"

Daniel fell to his knees and slid down the steep incline of the roof. Just as he hit the edge of the roof, his feet smashed into the gutter, stopping his slide. He lay there for a moment, panting, catching his breath, his heart thudding in his chest.

"You okay?"

Daniel lowered himself on to the ladder. "I'm not sure," he said, climbing down to the ground.

Together they went into the kitchen, and while Daniel patted cold water on his face, Nat raced around the house assembling a collection of pharmaceuticals. He managed to come up with a jar of Flintstone's vitamins for kids, Vick's Vaporub, a box of throat lozenges called Sucrets and an almost empty bottle of aspirin.

"Still breathing?" Nat asked.

Daniel was shaking, but he managed to nod. "I think so."

Nat opened the jar of vitamins. "Here. Take one of these." He studied the label. "It's got the complete US recommended daily allowance of vitamins and minerals. Can't hurt, right?"

Daniel shrugged. "I guess not."

"Which do you want?" He held out a handful of the brightly colored vitamins, each one shaped like a character from *The Flintstones* cartoon series. "There's Fred and Wilma and Dino and Pebbles."

Daniel grabbed one. "Who is this?"

"That's Wilma."

"Swell." He took the pill and popped it in his mouth, swallowing it instantly.

Nat winced. "Oh, well, I guess it's okay."

"I did something wrong?"

"Well, you're supposed to chew them."

"Oh."

"Try this one," said Nat. "It's a Fred."

Daniel crunched on the vitamin, chewing it carefully. "I feel better already."

In the new world in which Daniel found himself there was never a shortage of wonderful new things to examine. He found the compact-disc player particularly fascinating. The records he knew, the 78-rpm discs of his era, were three times the size of CDs and contained less than a tenth of the music.

Daniel held the shimmering disc up in front of his face and stared at himself in the silvery surface, trying to see the changes that he felt were taking place inside him.

"Hey." Claire was dressed in her white nurse's uniform. "Night shift tonight."

"That's tough."

"Nat told me what happened. Thanks for risking your life to save my underwear."

Daniel shook his head. "It wasn't anything. I just lost my balance, that's all."

Claire looked concerned for her mysterious house guest. "You sure? You could talk to John. He's a real good doctor. It wouldn't cost anything."

"It's not that. John seems very nice."

Claire smiled and nodded. "He is. He's the nicest man I know." She took the compact disc that he was holding and read the label. "Oh, hey, this is a great one. You like her?"

"Who doesn't like Billie Holiday?"

Claire slipped the disc into the player.

"You don't have to play it," said Daniel, quickly. He was almost pleading with her not to. Billie Holiday had been Helen's favorite singer.

"I'm going to play it quietly. Nat's asleep." She frowned at the player, as if not quite sure what to do with the disc.

"You have any idea how these things work? Do you want to put it on?"

"No," he said.

"I just got this CD player for my birthday. Some of the girls at work got it for me. But sometimes I think the old records sound better, don't you?"

Daniel nodded. "Yeah," he said, his voice low and husky.

Claire pressed a button, and the music, the smooth, sweet, high voice of Billie Holiday, drifted into the room. She sang "The Very Thought of You."

Daniel closed his eyes, forcing himself to listen but not immune to the pain of the memories that the music stirred up.

Claire didn't notice his emotion. She was fiddling with the player. "There's supposed to be some kind of EQ thing here – whatever EQ is – but I never know which of the buttons to press."

She turned and saw that something was going on inside Daniel, that he seemed to be on the verge of tears. Tentatively she reached out and touched his shoulder. She moved in closer until they were embracing.

The tears in Daniel's eyes welled up and trickled down his cheeks. Finally, for the first time, he gave in to his grief.

Claire stroked his hair and whispered softly in his ear. "You know, I know what it feels like. To lose someone. I know. I know how painful that can be."

They stood there, entwined in each other's arms,

listening to the music and to the remorse in Billie Holiday's voice, a mirror of the pain they both felt.

Daniel lowered his lips to hers and they kissed. She did not resist him or seem surprised by his action. It was a long, warm, comforting, consoling kiss, with a hint of passion lurking behind it. It was a physical expression of hope and sustenance, and he felt the comfort of trust and intimacy.

For a moment Daniel came alive like a spark in the darkest of nights. And for that brief moment he felt that he wasn't alone. Then the music filled his ears, and between their lips fell the shadow of Helen. Claire felt him tense and pull back.

"I'm sorry," said Daniel. "I'm . . . I'm not sure what –"

For a second Claire was angry, frustrated, embarrassed, yet some part of her understood what he was experiencing, knew that he had no desire to hurt her, that there was something else pressing down on him, something he had to resolve on his own.

But the kiss had comforted her too. "It's okay. It's, uh . . ."

"Claire, I don't know what I –" He was ready to let it all out, to trust her with his story. He was prepared to take a chance on her not believing him.

But she cut him off quickly, as if she couldn't stand to hear any stories or excuses from him. "I should get to work, I guess."

There was a long pause while she studied his anguished face. Then she gathered up her purse and went out, leaving Daniel standing in the middle of the room, listening to the Billie Holiday song fade, his heart on fire.

CHAPTER TWENTY

The rain of the day before had cleared and cleaned the air, and Daniel settled himself on the porch of the house in the darkness, savoring the cool, sweet night. He tried to calm himself down, attempting to think as clearly as he could about his problem. A new factor had been added to the complicated equation. He knew, he could feel, that he was undergoing some kind of physical change, and he doubted that it was for the better.

Daniel stared at his bandaged hand. Dots of blood were seeping through the dressing. A fleck marked the ridge of each knuckle.

When he had scuffed his knuckles on Fred's hard jaw Daniel really did not think much of it. Over the years, as a kid and later in the Air Corps, he had been in many scrapes and crack-ups and hardly ever had so much as a scar to show for them. He healed fast. His bones knit quickly.

He smiled grimly, ironically, at the thought that he had always considered himself immortal. Daniel knew that he looked the same as he had in 1939, but he felt different, as if he was slowing down, deteriorating slowly from the inside out.

So deeply was Daniel lost in thought, he didn't even notice John's car rolling to a halt at the curb. The slamming of the door broke his depressed reverie.

"John," said Daniel quietly. "Claire's not here. She had to work the night shift."

John advanced uncertainly. "I, uh, I guess I knew that already. I came to talk to you, Daniel."

"Me?"

John stood in front of Daniel, frowning, his eyes down, his lips pursed, as if trying to work out in advance what he was going to say. He paced back and forth for a few moments, then stopped and thought some more. Finally he spoke.

"Something is going on here. Something I need to straighten out. I have to settle this whole thing, otherwise I'm just going to go over it in my head until I can't think anymore." John began to pace again, as if movement helped him to think.

"What is it? What can I do?"

John stopped walking and turned back to Daniel. "You show up out of nowhere. A total mystery. No friends. No family. Nowhere to stay. All that is weird enough, right?"

"John, I know it sounds —"

John held his hand up, the flat of the palm out, as if he were a cop stopping traffic. "Next thing I know, Claire has you sleeping here."

"On the couch," said Daniel, quickly.

"Okay, okay. Look, I don't know if you know about this, but Claire and I have been dating. Last night wasn't the first time. It was the fourth or fifth time."

Daniel could see what was coming. "John —"

"Let me finish. You see, for the first time since I met her two years ago, things between us are feeling . . . maybe a little promising. And then you show up. How would you feel if you were in my shoes?"

"Lousy," admitted Daniel.

"Exactly. See, maybe it's coincidence, but suddenly

she doesn't smile at me like she used to. It seems like she's in a daze half the day. In a daze or too busy to have coffee with me at the coffee machine."

"The coffee what?"

"Machine. Vending machine, you know?"

"Oh yes, of course. Right."

John's brow was furrowed, and he stared at the ground, looking truly miserable. Daniel could certainly appreciate the feelings of any man who thought he might be on the verge of losing the woman he loved. "And maybe it's me, my imagination. But I'm not so sure. I know what you're thinking, but I've seen this before. You think things are going along great and then, *wham!*, it all falls apart. It only takes a second, and it has nothing to do with logic."

"I hear you," said Daniel softly. John could have been describing his life.

"I know what I am. I know what I'm like." He paused a moment as if what he had to say next was especially painful. "I know I'm no test pilot. I'm not . . . your type. Which happens to be *her* type. But I didn't realize I wasn't her type until you showed up. You see my problem?"

Daniel was working his bandaged fist into the palm of his left hand. "John –"

"I have no claim on Claire – except what I'm feeling, that is. So I'm only asking you to be honest with me." He took a deep breath. "If something is going on between you two, I need to know. Because, quite honestly, I hate being the underdog." He paused again. "Man, this is tough. So . . . is there anything between you and Claire?"

"Claire," said Daniel slowly, "Claire . . . is wonderful."

John's shoulders slumped, as if he knew that the bad news was coming. "I know she is. And I guess you found out about it too."

"But nothing is happening. *Nothing*."

John's eyes grew bright. "There isn't?"

"No. John, I'm in love with someone else. It's as simple as that."

John was split. On one hand, he was so happy with the news he had just received he wanted to dance a jig right there on the sidewalk, yet Daniel now seemed as sad as he himself had been a moment before. "I'm sorry."

"It doesn't really matter anymore. And you don't have to worry about me. I'll be leaving in the morning."

"Oh, well, you don't have to leave. Not on my account, anyway."

"I think I do," said Daniel firmly. "I think it's better for everybody."

John looked at him closely. The spots of blood on the bandage had grown in size in the few minutes they had been talking. He nodded toward Daniel's hand. "You know, you look like you're really bleeding there."

"Yeah. It's nothing."

"Want me to take a look at it?"

"It's okay. Thanks anyway."

John shook his head. "Well, I guess I'll . . ." He started toward his car.

Daniel watched him go, then he got up and walked quickly down to the sidewalk. "John, wait."

"Yeah?"

"I want to ask you something. Have you told Claire how you feel?"

"Well, not yet. I don't want to rush things. There's time yet, I guess."

Solemnly Daniel shook his head. "John, listen to me. You never know how much time there is. Do it now. Do it now before you regret it. Forever."

There was something in Daniel's voice that frightened John, a note of profound grief. In that second John realized that Daniel spoke from painful personal experience.

The instant John drove off, Daniel raced upstairs to Nat's room and woke the soundly sleeping boy.

"Nat," Daniel hissed. "Nat, wake up!"

Nat sat up, rubbing his eyes. "What is it?"

"Listen to me carefully. I was wrong. I was wrong about what I told you before."

Nat was still half asleep. "Wrong about what?"

"I was wrong about Alice."

The mention of his beloved's name woke Nat fully. "What? What about her?"

"You asked me what I would do, and I gave you completely the wrong idea. Nat, you have to tell her."

Nat sat upright in the bed. "How?"

"When you see Alice, the next time you see her, and your heart starts beating fast and you feel nervous . . . You know what I mean?"

"Of course I do! I hate that feeling."

"Well, when that happens let go."

"What do you mean, let go?"

"Just let go, and tell her how you feel. Tell her everything. All of it."

"*All* of it?"

"All of it. Those things you told me. All those

things you're feeling. Open your heart. Let it out. Sing to her."

Nat's eyes grew as wide and as round as hubcaps. He was so startled that he half expected his hair to stand up straight on his head. "You want me to . . . to *sing* to her!"

"Yeah!"

Daniel put his hands on the boy's shoulders and stared intently into his eyes. "Just tell her everything. Tell her immediately. Don't delay a minute, do you hear me? Tell her as soon as you can. Don't wait. Because you might never have the chance again. Do you understand?" Daniel lowered his voice and took a deep breath. "I was wrong. That's all. I thought you should know."

"Thanks," said Nat.

"Now go to sleep. Goodnight."

"'Night."

Nat lay back down, his spirits soaring after what Daniel had said. It sounded so right. It made sense.

In the bathroom Daniel carefully unwound the bandage on his hand and winced at what he saw. Blood, thick and turbid, dripped in a steady stream into the sink. The blood flow was stronger than when he had first hurt himself. The gashes looked much, much worse, raw and ragged. The skin was torn and was starting to turn black and blue. He ran the faucet and put his hand under the cool water. The wounds burned. Daniel gritted his teeth and flinched at the searing pain.

He was worried now and sick to his stomach. When would he know what was happening to him? How would he find out what *had* happened to him? He stared at his image in the mirror over the sink. "Oh, brother," he said to his reflection. "Ohhh, brother."

CHAPTER TWENTY-ONE

Nat wriggled and tossed in his bed, unable to sleep. His mind whirled; he was simultaneously tormented and exhilarated by Daniel's little speech, excited beyond belief at what he had heard. It was such a change of heart. That afternoon Daniel had sounded despondent, down on the entire world. Now he had come bursting into Nat's room with a whole new philosophy – one that Nat greatly preferred. It appealed to his romantic soul.

Nat lay still for a moment, wondering what he should do. His heart was pounding, and his skin was tingling. What had Daniel said? He had told him not to delay for a second, to tell Alice as soon as he could because there might not be a chance to do it some other time.

It sounded crazy, but Daniel had put such force behind his words. He had seemed so convinced, so emphatic. It occurred to Nat that a man who had been frozen for fifty years – and a test pilot to boot – would have a perspective on these matters different than that of ordinary mortals.

Nat made up his mind. He kicked aside the covers on his bed and jumped out, pulling on his clothes over his pajamas. Quietly he stole down the stairs and raced out into the night, running as fast as he could for Alice's house.

He had no idea what time it was – he had a feeling it was late – but he didn't care. Nat circled the house once and saw, to his delight, that the window of one room was half open. The curtains were rustling slightly in the evening wind, and the boughs of a gnarled apple tree curved out just under the sill.

"Do it," he whispered to himself. Nat knelt and grabbed a handful of pebbles from the gravel drive and stuffed them into the pocket of his trousers. Then he examined the tree. Being an eleven-year-old boy, Nat was something of a connoisseur of trees and how to climb them. This one would not be all that easy, but he was determined to try.

Nat swung himself up into the lower branches, struggling to reach the higher limbs. He was wearing his bedroom slippers, and they didn't grip the wood very well. Twice he slipped down the trunk, almost tumbling to the ground, but he hung on, climbing toward the top. When he was level with the bedroom window, he steadied himself and tossed some of the pebbles at the window. They pinged on the glass.

"Please don't let this be her parents' room," he muttered. Then he took a deep breath and burst into song.

The song he chose from his limited repertoire, the most romantic he knew, was "You Are My Sunshine." The sentiment was right on the money, as far as he was concerned.

"You are my sunshine, my only sunshine,"

Nat crooned at the top of his voice.

"You make me happy when skies are gray.
You'll never know, dear, how much I love you . . ."

Just as he got to the line "Please don't take my sunshine away," Alice appeared at the window of her room, rubbing the sleep from her eyes. She stared hard at the small boy singing in the tree-top a few feet away.

"Nat?" she gasped.

Nat stopped singing. "Alice!" he shouted. "I can't hold it in! I've got to tell you the truth! I've gotta let go!"

"Nat, what are you *doing*!" she screamed.

"I think about you all the time. I dream about you every night."

"You *what*?"

"I dream about you even when I'm awake! I hate summer 'cause I know I won't see you every day. And in school I swear I can smell you from across the classroom."

"You can do *what*?"

"No. I mean, your perfume. Whatever it is, it's the best. It's my favorite. And I write your name all over my books, and I say your name in my head all day!"

Lights appeared in the windows of the house next door. Alice glanced around worriedly. She tried to whisper and shout at the same time. "Nat! Have you lost your mind?"

Nat didn't care how he looked or who heard him. He was transported by the moment. "I've been wanting to tell you for the longest time!"

"Tell me what?"

"I've wanted to open up my heart to you. Alice – *I love you*!"

"*What*!" squeaked Alice.

Nat was giggling. He was giddy and lightheaded from the effect of his own words. "*I love you*!" he shouted.

130

"Be quiet!"

"There! It's out! Oh, and I wasn't really reading *Little Women*. Remember? In the library? But I will if it's something that's important to you."

"Nat! Please!"

> "The Greatest Love of All,
> Da-da, dum-dum-dum-da, dee-dee,
> Deedle-deedle . . ."

"Nat!"

> ". . . dum-dum, da-deeeeee,
> The Greatest –"

Red in the face, Alice slammed her window shut. Nat stopped singing abruptly.

For a moment he was bewildered, nonplused by the sudden silence. Then, love knowing no reason, he decided that her shutting the window was a good sign, that she was going to let him in. He shimmied down the tree and raced to the front door. He knocked and rang the doorbell.

Nat stood on the front step, eagerly waiting for his love to open the door to him. He saw a light come on in the house, and he straightened up, smoothing his hair and pasting a smile – actually, it was a grin – on his face.

The door swung open, and the grin vanished. Alice's father, rumpled with sleep, was standing there. He stared down at the small boy.

"This is a joke, right?"

Nat squared his shoulders. "No, sir. This is *very* serious."

"Is it?"

Nat nodded. "Yessir. I'm sorry to wake you up, but my name's Nat Cooper, and I'm in love with your daughter. I have been since kindergarten, and I want you to know –"

"Nat?"

"That's right, sir."

"Nat Cooper?"

"Yessir."

"Good night, Nat Cooper," said Alice's father. He slammed the door.

Nat stood there for a moment, staring at the door as if Alice's father were playing an elaborate practical joke on him. Then it dawned on him that the door was not going to open again.

Slowly, dejectedly, he turned from the door and slunk back the way he had come. At the sidewalk he stopped and looked back at the house.

And his heart leaped! All the life and love inside him rose like the sun. There she was at her bedroom window, staring down at him. Nat stared back. Very slowly a small, delighted smile crept across her face. Then she disappeared from the window. Nat looked at the spot where she had been and grinned a stupid little grin and then, with a jaunty spring in his step, bounced down the street.

"Daniel was right!" he whispered to himself. "Daniel was *right!*"

Nat was far from being the only person awake and busy in the town that night. At the airforce base a team of scientists was going over Harry Finley's capsule, which had been moved into one of the labs. Captain Wilcox paced nervously, watching the professionals measure every square inch, every bolt and rivet, of the mechanism. Teams of engineers, experts in the most esoteric fields, had been flying into the airbase for the last twenty-four hours, an avalanche of erudition that made Wilcox even more jittery.

It was his career here: that was what was on the line. He had had this character right in his office, and he had let him go. If they didn't find McCormick quick, then he, for one, was dead meat.

A lieutenant bustled up to him and saluted properly. Wilcox turned on him eagerly.

"What did you get?" Wilcox was waiting for McCormick's file, Finley's records, any shred of paper that might give him some sort of clue as to their whereabouts.

"Nothing yet, sir. It takes time to dig out these old records. It's been fifty years."

"I know that," the captain snapped. "Tell me something I don't know. This is highest priority. Tell G-2 to move it. We're not talking about spare tank parts here."

"They assure us we'll have the Blue File by morning, sir. They're aware of the situation."

"Aware? They better be more than that!" said Captain Wilcox angrily.

"They have no word yet, sir. But —"

Wilcox cut off his subordinate impatiently. "Get on the phone and tell G-2 that Doctor Cameron, the head of scientific research for the entire United States Air Force, is arriving from Washington at ten hundred. And not a minute too soon, if you ask me."

"Yessir!"

"And we have to find McCormick!"

"Yessir, absolutely. We're doing everything we can."

"Well, it's not enough." Wilcox thought for a moment, and then he had an idea. "The guy, McCormick, looked like he was in pretty terrible shape. I want an alert out to all the hospitals and doctors within a hundred miles. Tell them to be on the lookout for him."

"But what do we tell them?"

"I don't give a damn. Tell them he's armed and dangerous and is wanted by the FBI. Tell them that."

The lieutenant nodded. "But what about G-2? Shouldn't they be told?"

"Tell them what I just told you, lieutenant."

"Yessir."

Wilcox was red in the face. "And you can tell them this too: a whole branch of the FBI is arriving here in six hours, and if they can't locate this human ice cream by *yesterday*, we're gonna have a real serious problem. Got that?"

The lieutenant gulped. It was his turn to be nervous.

CHAPTER TWENTY-TWO

It was drizzling the next morning when Daniel slipped out of bed and dressed quickly in the gray light. The night before, after putting a fresh dressing on his damaged hand, he had sat down with a piece of paper and composed a note for Claire and Nat.

Words had never been Daniel's strong suit, and he had struggled for a long time to put his feelings and his fears down on this scrap of paper. He had re-read his note a hundred times and realized he would never be able to express all that he felt or explain all that had happened. He could do nothing more than to thank Nat and Claire from the bottom of his heart and move on.

Claire was still at work, her night shift drawing to a close, and Nat seemed to be out of the house. Daniel was relieved that neither mother nor son was home – it would be easier to leave without the pain of prolonged goodbyes. He stopped in the kitchen, attached his note to the refrigerator with a magnet and sighed heavily. He stared at the note as if it was his last will and testament, and for the thousandth time in two days he wondered what he was going to do next . . .

"You're leaving?"

Daniel turned. It was Nat. His hair was wet from the rain and he was jumpy, excited. He held a crumpled, damp, brown-paper bag under his arm.

Daniel nodded. "Yeah," he said. "I think it's better for me to be moving on."

Nat nodded, unhappy. He proffered the bag. "I got

this for you. I guess it's a kind of going-away present now. I didn't plan it that way, but . . ." He concluded with a little shrug.

"Nat." Daniel knew that the boy didn't have money to spend on presents for anybody.

"Take it. You might need it."

Daniel took the bag, reached in and pulled out a well-worn olive-drab Army Air Corps cotton flight jacket, *circa* 1939. For a moment Daniel could only gaze at the garment, tears welling in his eyes.

"It was nice of you to wake me up like that last night and everything. I got right out of bed and did what you said I should do."

"You did?"

Nat nodded. "I told her how I felt . . . how I feel. I sang a song and everything. I don't know how it worked, but at least she knows how I feel, right?"

"Right."

"So how's the jacket?"

Daniel slipped into the jacket, and for the first time in a long time he looked and felt like the Daniel of old. He squared his shoulders and stood up straight.

"Nat . . ."

"You like it? I got it at the thrift store. There was a leather one, but it cost too much."

"Leather was for show-offs." Daniel stroked the threadbare arms. "This is the real thing."

Nat was delighted. "Really? You mean I did the right thing? I got the right one?"

"Exactly. The right one." Daniel tapped Nat on the shoulder. "Well, I got the jacket. I got a co-pilot. Whadya say we do a little flying?"

*

Rain thrummed down on the treehouse roof, and thunder rumbled in the distance as a storm drew nearer.

"Low ceiling," said Daniel. "Bad visibility. But the B-25 can fly in any weather. And once we get up above the cloud line it'll be a bright summer day."

"Really?"

"Yep."

"Okay. Instrument check."

The interior of the treehouse had been converted into a makeshift copy of a B-25 cockpit. A baseball bat stood in as the steering yoke. A series of clocks scavenged from the house and an old bicycle speedometer were the fuel gauges, air-speed indicator, altimeter, compass and altitude reading. A rack of clothespins were the switches controlling the ship's electrical systems, and some old coathangers did double duty as the throttles and flap controls.

"Okay," said Daniel, deadly serious, as if this were the real thing. "Throttle open a half an inch. The mixture is rich. Gotta pump it into the system, get the oil to circulate. Got it so far?"

"Yeah," said Nat. He anxiously copied every move Daniel made, afraid of making a mistake.

"The carb heat is cold. That's bad. Fuel-injected engines have to be warm. Fuel shut-off is set to 'on.' Radio and electrical 'off.' They've gotta be off right now. Don't want a spark on all that fuel. Got that?"

"Uh-huh," said Nat, a trifle uncertainly.

"Sure?"

"Yeah. So far it's pretty much like a computer game. Ben has one. He's a kid from school."

"Okay. Circuit breakers in. Prime the engines a couple of pumps. Get that oil in there. Brake is set."

"Right," said Nat.

Daniel shook his head. "No, no. Always say 'Check.' 'Right' gets confusing."

Nat nodded. "I get it. Check."

"Okay, let's get started. Yell 'Prop clear.'"

"*Prop clear!*" shouted Nat.

"Turn on engines." Daniel pointed to the clothespins. "Right there. It's marked. Left engine first, then the right engine."

"Shouldn't that be port and starboard?"

Daniel shook his head. "Nope. Real pilots say left and right. Port and starboard gets confusing. Got it? Fire 'em up."

"Check." As Nat flicked at the switches, the thunder rumbled. If he didn't think about it too closely, he could almost imagine the big B-25 engines bursting into life.

"Watch your gauges. Make sure everything is copacetic, everything ship-shape. Oil pressure up, revs even. Watch the engine temperatures. Amps steady." Daniel's eyes studied the old alarm clocks, the kitchen clock, the mantel clock, and even he could see the needles dance and skip as power pumped into the great flying machine. "Does it all check out?"

"Check, check, check," said Nat.

"Okay. A little throttle. Easy. Now we're rolling. Test your controls." He vibrated the stick slightly. "Flight controls are free and correct. Radio and electrical on. That means you can talk to the tower."

Nat nodded. "Check, radio and electrical on."

"Now we're waiting for departure. He's up in the tower clearing the ships for take-off. Let him know you're here and ready to go."

"How do I do that?"

"Into your mike. Identify yourself. What's this ship called?"

"Uh . . . " Nat thought for a moment, and then a goofy grin spread across his face. "It's called Alice."

"It's got to be *something* Alice."

"Real Cool Alice."

"Good name," said Daniel, with a smile.

"Departure," said Nat. "This is B-25 Real Cool Alice requesting clearance for take-off."

"That's a roger, Real Cool Alice," said Daniel. "You are cleared for take-off on runway L-5." He turned to Nat. "Now, you say, 'Departure, I am with you.'"

"Departure, I am with you."

"That's a roger, cap. Good flying. Now say, 'Roger that, thanks, and over and out.'"

"Roger that, thanks, and over and out."

"Good. Throttle increase full. That's like putting on the gas a little. Flaps set for take-off – that's ten percent of flaps, okay?"

"Check."

"Now increase your back pressure."

"Check."

"Throttles open." Daniel raised his voice to be heard over the roar of the engines, and Nat could have sworn that the treehouse was moving, rushing across his yard, all the yards on the street, suburban lawn after suburban lawn knitting together to provide a runway for his aircraft.

"Cruise climb," ordered Daniel. "Feel the lift? Feel the air under your wings?"

"Check!" yelled Nat. "Absolutely check!"

"Okay. We're up. We're flying. Bring your landing gear up and lock. A light will come on in the panel to let you know that it's in."

"Check. Gear up and lock." Nat could swear he could see a light burning ruby-red on the instrument panel.

The undercarriage folded into the treehouse with a little shuddering motion, and speed increased.

"Okay. Now we circle around the airfield one turn, and they'll check from the ground and let us know if our tail is on fire or anything."

"What?" squeaked Nat.

"It's a joke."

"Check."

"Can you see the field?"

Nat glanced out of the treehouse. "Yeah, uh, check. It's over there."

"Good. Let's make a turn." Daniel leaned to his left, as did Nat. He could feel the plane slip easily through the damp air, the propellers pulling them along.

"Smooth," cautioned Daniel. "Keep it smooth."

The storm was almost on them now, and there was a bright flash of lightning – it was so close, it seemed to be right there in the cockpit with them – followed by the loud roar of thunder.

Daniel studied the gauges. "Okay. Okay. We've lost an engine. But don't panic. We've got another one."

"*What*? What do we do?"

"Feather the prop! Cut the fuel! Fast!"

Nat's little fingers flew over the switches. "Check."

"Okay. Give her a little rudder. That's it. That's it. Now let's look for a place to put her down."

Nat pointed. "Look! There's a field."

"Looks good. Okay. Stay calm. Nose down. Speed down."

"Check."

"Optimum glide speed. We do one pass over the field and pull power back. Get the flaps in a notch."

His heart in his mouth, Nat glanced over at Daniel, concentrating on the controls. "Are . . . are we going to make it?"

"Put the landing gear down."

"Check," said Nat.

"Mixture rich, carb heat is on, more flaps. Watch the horizon. Nat, watch the horizon."

"Pull back on the stick?"

"Pull back. Don't flare. Grease her in. Watch the horizon! Watch the horizon!"

Nat could sense that their wheels were just inches from the ground. Very carefully he dropped the stick and the plane dipped down to earth. There was a bump as they touched down.

"Reverse engines. Flaps up."

The engines roared in contrary motion, and the flaps flipped up, breaking the rush of air over the wings, slowing them down.

"Pull back on the brakes. *Slowly* now. Slowly. That's it. Nice and easy."

The big plane rolled to a complete stop on the wet grass. The only sound was the patter of rain on the treehouse roof. Gradually the switches became clothespins; the throttles returned to their earthly form, coathangers; the yoke became a baseball bat again. But Nat didn't care. He was agog, amazed at what he had just accomplished.

"Wow," he said, awestruck.

Daniel sat, motionless, staring ahead of him, remembering the first time he had set a B-25 down. It was so long ago. But right then he felt as if it had been only yesterday. "If you can land a B-25, you can do anything," he said softly. "Hear me? Anything."

Nat and Daniel looked at each other for a moment. "Thanks for the jacket." And he wanted to say: *And thanks for letting me fly my plane one last time.*

"You're welcome."

"I better be running along," said Daniel. He uncoiled himself from the cramped position, stretched and started to get out of the treehouse. He put one foot on the ladder.

"Hey," said Nat, a little desperately. "You sure you don't wanna stay? Stay for just a coupla more days. You can't leave today. The weather is lousy. It's almost lunchtime. Mom'll be home soon. Stay for lunch. What would you like for lunch? How about it?"

Daniel stopped and grinned. "Nat, there's nothing I would rather do."

Nat allowed himself to hope. "There isn't? Then why don't you do it?"

"But . . . "

Nat's thin shoulders slumped. "There's always a but, isn't there? When you grow up that's how things are."

But Daniel didn't answer. He had gone very pale, and beads of sweat were popping out on his forehead. He seemed to be having trouble holding on to the ladder.

"Daniel?"

Daniel's eyes blurred. "Nat?" And then he fell as if toppling into infinite darkness.

CHAPTER TWENTY-THREE

Nat jumped out of the treehouse and kneeled next to Daniel. Daniel was sprawled in the wet grass, his eyes open but unseeing. A violent, bone-shaking tremor rocked his body as convulsions ripped through him.

"Daniel! What's happening!"

Daniel's jaw worked, opening and closing as he tried to speak, but no sound came, just the sharp rasping of painful breathing.

"*Daniel*!" Nat looked around, bewildered. Then tears began pouring from his eyes, a tortured wail breaking from his throat. He was scared, confused. He didn't know what to do. But he knew his friend was dying.

Nat ran into the rain, panicked and weeping. He darted into the street. A car bore down on him, horn blaring.

"Wait!" screamed Nat. "Stop!"

"Crazy kid!" yelled the driver.

Another car screeched to a halt in the rain-swept street. The driver vaulted out of the car, yelling at the top of his lungs. His passenger followed him out into the rain.

"*Are you out of your mind? What the hell are you doing? If your mother told you to play in traffic, I'm sure she didn't mean it literally* . . . Nat! You *maggot*!"

Nat had never been so deliriously happy to see Steven in his entire life.

One look from Felix, and he could see that his

friend was in very bad shape. "Nat!" He shouted. "What's goin' on?"

"*Hurry up! It's an emergency!*" Nat was frantic, beside himself with fear. He raced for his back yard, Felix and Steven right on his heels.

Nat dropped to his knees next to Daniel and put his ear to his chest, listening for a heartbeat. "We gotta take him to the hospital!"

"Who the hell is he?" asked Steven, his hands on his hips, a sceptical look on his face.

"He's a friend. Come on! Let's get moving. He's *dying*!"

But Steven didn't budge. "Wait a minute. A friend? Who exactly is he?"

Nat had taken just about all he could stand. He drew himself up to his full four feet, got up close to Steven and, right in his face, screamed at the top of his small lungs. "*He's the frozen guy we told you about!*"

Felix paled. He couldn't believe that Nat was letting the cat out of the bag, and to his brother Steven, of all people.

"Frozen?" said Steven.

"*Yes. He's the frozen guy! And he's top-secret and real sick, and if you don't help us take him to the hospital right now, I'm gonna tell the Air Force and the CIA and the President that it was your fault, and they'll throw you in jail for the rest of your life! Now help me carry him to the car, asshole! Now!*"

The only person more surprised by this spirited outburst than Steven was Nat himself.

Steven drove faster than he had ever driven in his life, covering the few miles to the hospital in no time flat.

144

He drew up in front of the emergency-room entrance, his tires squealing. The three boys staggered under the weight of Daniel as they hauled him into the emergency room.

The nurse on duty at the front desk took one look at Daniel's convulsing body and swung into action. She grabbed a microphone on her desk. "ER-5: we've got a code one. Trauma team!"

Everything seemed to happen at once. Orderlies and doctors appeared from nowhere. Daniel was slapped on to a cart, and a team of doctors converged on his body like piranhas.

"Collapse and crushing chest pain," intoned one of the nurses. Needles and tubes slid into Daniel's veins, and a tube went down his throat.

"Blood pressure?" asked a doctor.

"One-fifty over ninety, pulse one-twelve and thready. He's diaphoretic."

"Let's get some blood. I want a count and gases."

"He's gotta get to intensive care now. Let's move it, people."

Just as an oxygen mask was slipped over Daniel's face John, the doctor attending, glanced at his patient. "Oh, my God," he said.

Daniel was rushed down the corridor toward the intensive-care unit. Nat, Felix and Steven watched too. Nat felt as if a little piece of his heart had been chiseled off.

In intensive care the doctors and nurses did their best to stabilize Daniel's condition, trying to keep him alive long enough to get the test results back. At this stage the doctors had no idea what was wrong with him.

As it turned out, the tests didn't help much either.

John puzzled over the computer printouts, unable to make any sense of the numbers and symbols. In all his years of practicing medicine he had never seen anything like this. He rushed down the hall to the office of the head of medicine, Dr Sullivan, a medical man twice the age of, and twice as experienced as, John.

Sullivan was on the phone when John burst into his office. The doctor looked at his colleague's face and hung up immediately. "John, what's the matter?"

John thrust the papers under Dr Sullivan's nose. "These are from McCormick in intensive care."

"McCormick! The FBI just called and told me that he's in some kind of trouble. They said he was dangerous."

"He's in danger of dying," said John. He paced the room, agitated. "I'm a little confused by these results. What kind of blood activity is this?"

Sullivan dropped his glasses on to his nose and scanned the papers quickly. "This is *blood* activity."

Nat went in search of his mother. He found her just before she went off duty. It had been a long and tiring shift, and fatigue showed in her eyes. She looked startled and frightened when she saw her son.

"Nat! What's the matter?" She dropped to her knees and seized him by the shoulders.

"It's Daniel," said Nat. He was fighting back tears.

"Daniel? What happened?"

"He's sick. Real sick."

"What? Where? *Here*?"

Nat nodded. "Mom, I'm gonna tell you something . . . but you have to promise not to think I'm completely crazy. Okay?"

Claire felt numb, but she managed to nod.

Nat took a deep breath. "Remember I told you that Felix and I . . . Remember I told you we found a frozen guy?"

Claire nodded.

"The frozen guy . . . is Daniel."

"Daniel?"

"Daniel got frozen in 1939. He got thawed out by accident. By us. Last Thursday."

"I can't believe it."

"Mom," said Nat solemnly. "I'm not making this up."

Claire studied her son's serious face and knew, in that instant, that he was telling the truth. She smoothed his hair and kissed him. "I believe you, honey."

Daniel lay, scarcely moving, in the intensive-care unit, listening to the sounds of the machines around him. The beeps and whirrs and clicks were soft and quiet, but they scared him none the less. Intravenous tubes ran into his arms, and pressure patches were stuck on his chest and skull, eavesdropping on his insides. He felt less than human, as if he was now nothing more than part of a larger, soulless machine.

His skin was ashen. His cheeks were sunken and his lips parched, and he was tired almost to death. He looked older. Gray hair sprouted at his temples.

Claire suppressed the tears she felt coming on. Instead she forced herself to smile. "Hey," she said softly, "didn't I tell you to quit following me?"

Daniel opened his eyes and tried to smile. "My superior officers always said I was insubordinate."

"They were right." Claire blinked back a tear.

"Did Nat tell you?"

Very slowly Claire nodded, then shook her head. "It's not possible. It *can't* be."

There was a note of resignation in Daniel's voice. "Claire, I was born in 1909. I remember World War I, the Roaring Twenties, the Depression. I remember them as if they were yesterday. I lived them. I remember things that you have only read about in history books."

Tentatively she put out her hand and touched the swatch of gray hair at his temple. "Daniel, *please*." Tears detached themselves from her eyes and rolled down her cheeks. "I can't believe it."

He nodded weakly. "I know. I know. That's how I felt when Harry told me about his idea." Daniel smiled slightly, as if to himself. "Harry was a great guy. I wish you had known him. I wish I could find him. He would know what to do."

Claire stared at him. "Harry? Harry . . . Finley?"

Daniel started as if he had been pinched. He looked at her, amazed. "How do you know? Did Nat . . .?"

Claire shook her head quickly. Then, distraught, she ran a hand through her hair. "Oh, God. A woman called yesterday. She left a message. I thought it was a wrong number. I'm sure the message is still on the machine."

"A woman? Who? Was her name Blanche?"

Claire shook her head. "She didn't say. She just said that she knew Harry Finley and left a number."

There were two little spots of color on Daniel's cheeks now, and there seemed to be more strength in his limbs. The machines picked it up, beeping a little louder. Recording needles jumped on the graph paper.

"Claire," begged Daniel, "you have got to help me.

Help me get out of here. We have to go back to your house and get that number out of the machine."

Claire smiled. "No, well, see, you don't have to do that. You can just call the machine, punch in a code and the machine will play the message for you."

Despite the danger of the moment Daniel still found time to admire a good piece of technology. "A machine does all that? That's amazing. You go make the calls. I'll get dressed." He started struggling out of the bed.

"But, Daniel, you're ill."

His gaze held hers. "Claire, I *have* to do this. Do you understand me? I *have* to do it."

Claire thought for a second or two. "I'll go make the calls. Then I'll be right back to help you."

The Lear jet touched down at the air base right on time, and Captain Wilcox was waiting on the tarmac to greet Cameron, the scientist sent from Washington to oversee the investigation into the Project B (for Buford) fiasco.

He appeared in the doorway of the jet, looking a little shaken. He walked down the steps unsteadily, almost tripping and falling half way down.

Wilcox rushed over to him. "I'm Wilcox, sir. Are you feeling okay?"

Cameron shrugged. "I'm not the best flier, that's all. But I hear you have some good news."

Wilcox grinned broadly. "Yessir, we have some *real* good news. I am very pleased to be able to tell you that we've got Lieutenant McCormick in a hospital bed." Wilcox cackled. "And his wandering days are done. They've got so many wires on that guy, he's trussed up like a Thanksgiving turkey."

CHAPTER TWENTY-FOUR

Outside the intensive-care unit John and Claire almost ran smack into each other.

"Claire! What the hell is going on? Daniel has some form of accelerated leukemia – I've never seen anything like it. No one's ever seen anything like it. It's bizarre."

"We have to get him out of here," said Claire firmly. "We don't have much time."

"Claire, you can't be serious! Sullivan just told me that the FBI is on the way here. Daniel's in some sort of trouble, and they want to talk to him in the worst way."

Claire shook her head. "Daniel's not in any trouble. At least, he's not a criminal or anything like that. But we *have* to move him."

"But the FBI!" protested John.

"Forget about them. John, you have to trust me on this. Please."

"What can I do?"

"*Stall them.*"

John didn't stop to think about what he did next. He didn't bother to pace and ruminate for as much as a second. He just reached out, grabbed Claire and kissed her, deeply, intensely, passionately. He telegraphed his love for her through his lips until she really got the message. When he let her go she tottered back a couple of steps, a quiet, happy smile on her face.

"Hurry!" said John.

Claire raced back into the intensive-care unit and began pulling the electrodes off Daniel's chest. She disconnected the IV in his arm and capped it.

"Okay, time to get out of bed."

Slowly, painfully, Daniel swung out of the bed and began getting dressed. His fingers were numb and unresponsive, and the buttons on his shirt defeated him.

"Here, let me." Claire did the buttons up quickly and then helped him into his flight jacket.

Nat appeared from the corridor, rolling a wheelchair in front of him. "Get in."

Daniel lowered himself into the chair, and the three of them took off down the corridor of the hospital, trying to beat the clock. At a corner they stopped, and Nat peeked around the next corner to the elevators.

The passageway was full of men in Air Force uniforms and guys who looked like the FBI agents he had seen on television. They were all fanned out around Wilcox and Cameron.

Nat didn't have to be told – he knew the enemy when he saw it. "Oooops! Not that way, Mom."

"The elevator!" She turned to the bank of freight elevators. "Nat, go hit the down button!"

John was well aware of the part he had to play. He threw himself into the middle of the knot of military men and scowling feds. "I'm Doctor Halsy," said John. "There is something you should know . . ."

Wilcox tried to brush him off like a pesky puppy. "I'm sorry, we're in a rush here."

"It's very important."

Cameron stopped, always ready to extend professional courtesy to a fellow medical man. "What is it, doctor?"

"If you're looking for McCormick, he's been moved to the east-wing intensive care." He pointed down the corridor, the way they had come. "First right down the east corridor, third door on the left. Room 144."

"Why, thank you, doctor."

"Let's go," growled Wilcox, leading his men down the hallway, as if at the head of a squad of cavalry.

John slumped against the institutional green wall of the corridor and breathed heavily. He took off his glasses and fanned himself. "The things you do for love," he muttered.

John gave good directions. The thundering herd of government men rushed down the passageway and found room number 144 without trouble. They blasted through the double swinging doors and stopped dead in their tracks. They all glanced around, astonishment plain on their faces.

"The doctor said this was intensive care."

"Well, it isn't," said a passing nurse. "It's the cafeteria."

"What the hell is going on here?" demanded Wilcox.

"Looks like lunch," said one of the federal agents.

The elevator dropped down seven floors to the underground parking lot, and Claire, Daniel and Nat piled into the family station wagon. Claire hit the gas, and the car roared out of the garage and zoomed through the streets of the town. Instead of heading for home,

Claire took a different route, aiming for a more affluent, better-kept neighborhood than they lived in.

The car came to a halt in front of a well-cared-for old house on a quiet side street. Daniel still looked ill, and he seemed to be growing older by the minute, but he didn't care anymore. He got out of the car and was the first to reach the door, scarcely noticing the steep porch steps, and rang the bell several times.

It was answered by a middle-aged woman, who appeared to be in her early fifties. She was startled to see a wild-eyed old man on her doorstep, accompanied by a small boy and a woman in a nurse's uniform.

Daniel stared at the woman for a moment and decided she wasn't Blanche – Blanche would be much older – but she did look familiar. There was something about her, but he couldn't quite put his finger on it . . .

"Yes? Can I help you?"

"I'm looking for Harry Finley," said Daniel. "He was a scientist. His wife was Blanche Finley. They were both from Chicago. Do you know this man? Please say you do."

The woman smiled but still looked puzzled. "Yes, I know him. I believe that's my father you're talking about. I'm Susan Finley. At least, that was my maiden name."

"Your *father*?" Then it struck him. Of course! That day at the picnic when Blanche and Harry had announced that they were going to have a baby. No wonder she looked familiar. "Your father! Is he home?"

Susan Finley's eyes were downcast, as if David had found an old bruise and pressed hard. "I'm sorry . . . but my father is dead."

"Dead?" whispered Daniel. For a moment he stood stock-still, then his face fell and he sank slowly down on to the porch bench, staring straight ahead. He looked shattered.

"He lived here once . . . for a couple of months . . . but he died before I was born. You must be looking for another man."

Daniel shook his head. "No. There's no mistake. I was . . . his best friend."

Susan Finley moved closer. Her eyes narrowed, staring at him as if seeing him for the first time . . . as if she was seeing a ghost.

"Daniel?" she said.

It didn't take Wilcox and his cohorts long to figure out what was going on. They headed out of the hospital, making for the parking lot, Wilcox consulting a bulging blue file as he strode along.

"Susan Finley's address is 14, Blue Cypress Pond Road. Blue File says her father discovered a problem two months after McCormick volunteered. Finley died in a chemical fire, trying to save this guy. Apparently, he was a friend of his."

The FBI agents brought the cars around to the front of the hospital, and they all piled in, doors slamming and engines racing. Wilcox and Cameron settled in the back of a limousine and continued to look over the file.

"G-2 Operations claimed McCormick was killed as well. They closed his file. There was no investigation. The project slipped through the cracks when the war started. In the chaos after Pearl Harbor, I guess. It was completely forgotten."

Cameron looked shocked. "You mean to tell me he was lost? McCormick was just *misplaced*? Misplaced for fifty years? He sat there all that time and no one noticed? I can't believe it. It's too crazy."

Wilcox winced. This whole thing *was* crazy, and he really knew it. He had met McCormick first-hand. "That's, uh . . . how it looks, sir. The inventory had the capsule marked down as a heavy-duty industrial water heater." And no one — except for Wilcox — would ever know how close they had come to junking the damn thing, how close they had come to selling the copper for scrap.

Cameron shook his head in disbelief. "Oh, my God."

Susan Finley had inherited all of her father's papers and journals, and her mother had bequeathed bulging family albums of photographs and letters. She and Daniel, trailed by Nat and Claire, trooped down to the cellar and began sorting through cartons of old papers, looking for something, a clue, a hint of what had happened all those years ago. They raised clouds of dust as they worked, sifting through the scraps of the past.

"My mother used to talk about you, Daniel," Susan said. "She mentioned the experiment more than once, though she didn't know much about it." She corraled a stray wisp of hair and wiped a smudge of dust from her chin. "You know, he did everything he could to fix his mistake . . ."

"It wasn't his fault," said Daniel.

"Maybe not, but he felt that it was."

Suddenly Daniel wasn't listening anymore. In one

of the boxes he had discovered a stack of journals bound in red leather. In his memories of Harry Daniel always saw him with one of those red journals under his arm. The shock of recognition almost overwhelmed him. Carefully he opened volume number one. The faded old pages pulled away from their binding. Harry had recorded every phase of the experiment in his tiny, crabbed handwriting.

"November 26, 1939," Daniel read aloud. "Zero-four-seventeen-hundred hours. Test commenced."

Quickly Daniel flipped a few pages forward and read intently. It seemed that Harry had realized almost immediately that the experiment was in trouble. He had run some side tests on laboratory animals and recorded his disappointing results in the logs, his handwriting growing more untidy and more frantic as experiment after experiment failed. Daniel had never been too clear on the hard science of Harry's work, so the jumble of detailed equations meant little to him, but the notes in the comments column told him all he needed to know. "Uncontrollable rapid aging . . . molecular disintegration . . . exoskeletal breakdown . . . Aging irreversible . . ."

Daniel closed the book, raising a small puff of brownish dust. "Irreversible," he said, his voice hollow. "Irreversible."

Claire tried to slip her arms around him, to hold him and give him what little comfort she could, but he shook free of her. "Daniel, maybe we should go back to the hospital. Maybe there's something they can do?"

Susan Finley nodded. "Take my father's notes and see what they can make of them. Who knows what's changed in fifty years? Maybe they can help now."

Very slowly Daniel shook his head. He stared down into the cardboard box, then he reached in and extracted an old, yellowed, dog-eared black-and-white photograph and gazed at it, holding it lightly in his hands as if it was something sacred and fragile, something that might disintegrate. The picture was of Helen and a little girl, someone he could not identify.

Claire peered over his shoulder and understood everything. "That's her, isn't it?"

Daniel's nod was almost imperceptible. "Helen," he said huskily.

"Is . . . Is that your little girl?"

Daniel shook his head, his eyes still fixed on the picture. "No. We were never married."

"That's me," said Susan Finley. "I think I was about two years old when that was taken."

"That can't be," said Daniel. "Helen died almost a year before you were born."

Susan Finley looked puzzled. "No. She didn't die. I remember Mother saying something about Aunt Helen being in an accident —"

"A car accident," insisted Daniel. "It was before you were born."

"I know that, but . . ."

The photograph slipped from Daniel's fingers. "But what?"

Susan Finley shrugged. "She's alive."

For a moment they all feared that Daniel would faint. The blood drained from his face, and he staggered a few steps, his chest heaving in an attempt to catch his breath. "Where? Where is she?" he gasped.

"She retired," said Susan Finley. "Up north. Point Reyes."

"That's where we grew up! That's where the light-house is!" shouted Daniel.

Susan nodded vigorously. "I know, I know. She used to talk about you. About how you went to school together."

"And she's there now?" said Daniel.

"I . . . I guess so," said Susan. "I haven't spoken to her for a couple of months. But . . . ."

Daniel turned to Claire and held her by the shoulders. "Claire, you've done so much for me already, but I have to ask for your help one more time. Help me get to her. I've got to see her once more . . . for the last time."

"Let's move it!" said Claire.

They had to help Daniel up the cellar stairs. Once outside, he moved slowly towards Claire's car. Nat supported him on one side, Susan on the other.

"When did she move to Point Reyes?" Daniel asked.

"About seven years ago. She retired there after Uncle Charlie died . . . her husband."

Daniel stopped dead in his tracks. "She was married?"

Susan hated to be the one to break the news to the old man. "I'm . . . Yes, she was."

Daniel lowered his head. "I guess that was to be expected. Why would she wait for me?"

Susan smiled through the tears that had sprung into her eyes. "She never forgot you. I know that for a fact."

"How?" Nat helped Daniel into the front seat of the car and slammed the door. Daniel leaned out of the window. "How do you know she never forgot me?"

"They had a son. They named him Daniel."

Nat was looking down the street. A procession of official-looking cars was headed in their direction. "Let's get out of here."

"Right!" said Claire, gunning the engine. The car refused to move. "Oh, no!"

"Mom, I think you should put the car in drive."

"Oh, right."

Daniel touched Susan's hand. "Your father was a great man, Susan. Never forget that."

"I won't," said Susan, with a little smile.

"Let's go!" Nat shouted.

The car peeled away from the curb, flying down the street. "Seatbelts!" shouted Claire.

CHAPTER TWENTY-FIVE

Claire put her foot down, and her car bucked forward, heading straight for the military convoy descending on Susan Finley's quiet suburban street. The lead car of the formation saw Claire bearing down on them and stamped on the brake, throwing the vehicle into a 180-degree turn, the other cars behind fanning out, creating a makeshift road block.

But Claire had made up her mind that nothing was going to stop her. Instead of slowing down, she hit the gas and roared straight at the blockade.

"Mom, are we going as fast as we can?" yelled Nat.

"What do you want from me? I'm trying, Nat! I'm trying."

It took a second or two for Wilcox and his men to realize that the car was not going to stop. When it finally dawned on them they dove for cover, throwing themselves out of the path of the onrushing vehicle. Claire was driving like a pro, slaloming from side to side, threading her way through the roadblock, her tires screaming.

In a flash they were through, but Daniel knew they were not in the clear. The Air Force, the FBI and the local police could mobilize thousands of pursuers. It was only a matter of time before they ran him to earth – and time was the one thing he did not have.

"Claire," said Daniel, "I need an airplane."

Claire shot him a glance. "Are you crazy? Where am I supposed to get an airplane?"

"I'm not going to make it in this car. They're going to get us long before I get to her."

"But where –?"

"The air show," said Nat in a small voice. "There are planes there."

Daniel and Claire exchanged a look.

"Oh, boy," said Claire. "Nat, hold on. You too, Daniel." She pressed the gas pedal to the floor and the car leaped forward, rocketing through traffic.

Hanging on for dear life though he was, Nat was delighted at his mother's daring. "Mom! All right, Mom! Way to drive!"

Daniel was amazed too. "Holy cow, you drive just like I used to."

About ninety seconds later they got to the entrance of the airport where the air show was being held. Claire zoomed up to the gate and screeched to a stop. The security guard on the gate leaned in toward the driver's-side window.

"Got a pass?" he asked.

Claire flashed him her most winning smile. "Just dropping off a pilot."

"Sorry, ma'am, but –" That was as far as he got.

Claire glanced in her rearview mirror and saw the military convoy bearing down on them. "Gotta go!" she said. She punched the accelerator and zoomed through the open gate, racing out on to the tarmac.

The air show was in full swing, the grandstands packed with people, the sky full of planes. Claire raced over to the B-25 and stopped. "There's your ride."

Daniel turned in the seat and touched Nat on the cheek. "Thanks,' he said. "Thanks for bringing me this far."

Nat tried to smile, but he couldn't. His head sank between his shoulders, and his eyes were downcast and gloomy.

Claire jumped out of the car. "Stay here," she ordered her son. "Don't move."

Casually, as if they were just a couple out for a day at the air show, Claire and Daniel ambled over to the B-25, gawking like tourists.

Daniel tapped the crew chief on the shoulder. "Say, sonny, can I take a look inside?"

"Sure thing," said the man, hardly glancing at him.

Daniel turned to Claire. "Remove those wheel blocks and I'll never ask for another favor."

"Why stop now?" she said, smiling. Then she threw her arms around him and hugged him close. "Look, I'll see you around, one way or another."

"Hey," Daniel whispered in her ear, "you're holding my heart!"

She pushed him toward the plane. "Go."

Daniel climbed into the aircraft, made his way to the cockpit and sat in the pilot's seat. There was no time for an instrument check. He had to assume that the crew kept the machine in tip-top condition.

"Prop clear!" Daniel yelled. The engines coughed once, blew a puff of blue smoke, then burst into life.

"Hey!" yelled the ground-crew chief. "What the hell are you doing?" The man was running after the errant bomber, but Daniel was already off the apron, headed for the start of the runway. A few moments later he was in the air . . .

Claire watched him soar into the sky and stared after him until the big airplane was just a speck on the horizon. She turned back to her car. Doctor Cameron and Wilcox were standing there, backed up by a wall of FBI and Air Force muscle.

"Mrs Cooper," said Wilcox. "I think you may be under arrest."

Claire shrugged. "It doesn't matter anymore. How about I trade you?"

"Trade? Trade what?" demanded Wilcox.

"Don't arrest me." She opened the trunk of the car and they saw the stack of journals. "And I'll give you all the information you ever needed. Everything you'd ever want to know about freezing someone."

Cameron's eyes grew wide. "My God! Are these Harry Finley's notebooks? Where did you get them?"

But Claire wasn't listening. She was staring into her car, pale and trembling. "Oh, my God," she whispered, terror pulsing through her. "Where's my son?"

Daniel took the plane up to the service ceiling altitude of 24,000 feet and settled the velocity at the 230 miles per hour cruising speed. And he set there, hugging the coast, heading north, flying toward a too long delayed date with his past.

But the effort of getting the big aircraft off the ground had sapped him of much of his ebbing strength. It was all he could do to keep the B-25 level and on course. He sat back in the pilot's seat and closed his eyes for a moment, trying to focus, desperately striving to pump some strength into his tired old body.

From behind him he heard a sound, the noise of a fire extinguisher falling from its wall mount, clanging to the metal floor, loud enough to be heard over the roaring twin engines. Daniel opened his eyes and turned in his seat, surprised by the intense pain that so small an action caused him. He gaped as his gaze fell on Nat.

"Oh, no," he groaned. "Nat. Oh, no. Your mother is going to be crazy with worry."

Nat was crouched in the bombardier's well, his eyes big and excited, yet afraid at the same time. Of course, he knew that Daniel wasn't going to turn around and take him back, but he didn't want him to get angry at him either.

"What . . . What are you doing here?"

"You didn't even say goodbye," said the boy.

CHAPTER TWENTY-SIX

Cameron almost dove into the trunk, dying to get his hands on the lost journals of Harry Finley. He grabbed the first red-jacketed volume and devoured it with his eyes, finding enough data in a single page of notes to answer a dozen thorny scientific and theoretical questions that had plagued him for years.

"This is amazing! The man was a genius. If only I could have been there when he was working on this!"

Claire didn't give a damn about science. All she wanted was her son back, safe and sound. Suddenly she felt exhausted. A case of hysterics was ready to burst forth. Claire was sick of adventure – she wanted to go back to her quiet, safe, dull little world.

Wilcox was jabbering into a cellular phone, issuing orders and then countermanding them, not quite sure what to do.

"Can we talk to them?" Claire asked. "Can we get the plane on the radio?"

"They're not transmitting," Wilcox said. "We have them on radar. They're headed north. That's all we know for sure right now."

Cameron shut the notebook with a loud snap. "Wilcox, there's a change of plan."

"Yessir?"

"I'm going back to the capsule. I want to study it in detail with these notes handy. Call Doctor Reeves and get him out here immediately."

"Yessir!"

"I also want you to get on to the hospital. Get them to fax me all the data they took on McCormick. I want everything – serial EKG, cardiac enzymes, the works. Understand?"

"Yes, sir. But what about the plane?"

Cameron shrugged. "The plane is of no importance."

"No importance!" yelped Claire. "How can you say that? My son is on that plane."

Cameron smiled. "I'm sorry. The plane is of no importance to *me*. Wilcox, as soon as it lands, and wherever it lands, I want an escort to take Mrs Cooper to get her son." Cameron turned to go, then stopped and turned back. "Needless to say, there is no question of criminal charges."

"Thank you," said Claire more grateful that Nat would be returned to her than at the dropping of charges. "Thank you very much."

"No," said Cameron. "Thank *you*," he tapped the folder in his hands, "for this."

In the time it took the B-25 to travel a few hundred miles to the north Daniel raced ahead. Nat, sitting in the co-pilot's seat, watched worriedly as his friend aged rapidly, his shoulders rounding, his back hunched. His face became lined and sunken, his hair snowy-white, his hairline receding and thin on top. His eyes grew watery and rheumy. Pains were shooting through his limbs, and his hands and feet felt heavy as if his bones had turned to lead.

"Daniel? Are you all right?"

Daniel closed his eyes and nodded. "Yeah. I'm okay." Slowly he opened his eyes again and stared out of the window, looking down at the rugged Californian coastline. He smiled a serene smile of contentment.

"Look . . ."

Beneath them Nat could see bluffs and a beach pounded by a wild surf. On the cliffs stood a lighthouse painted a candy-striped red and white, then a stretch of field and the old keeper's house a few hundred yards away.

"It looks exactly like it always did." Daniel tried to shift to get a better look, and he winced in pain as he did so. There were tears in his eyes, but they were tears of wonder and happiness.

Daniel put his hands on the steering yoke and, slowly and painfully, pushed the airplane into a banking turn, an easy downward spiral, dropping in altitude by several hundred feet in a matter of seconds. His arthritic fingers curled on the controls, and with great effort he throttled back, bringing the air speed down, the nose level and true. The B-25 was settled on approach, dropping from the sky for the green grass of the field on the cliffs.

But Daniel knew he didn't have the strength. He could feel the energy flowing from him like a vat draining.

"Nat." Daniel reached out and placed the boy's hand on the steering yoke. "You have to help me."

Nat swallowed hard and tried to quell his fear. "Help? *Me?* Help *you?*"

Daniel nodded. "You have to put her down."

Nat gripped the steering yoke tight, his knuckles curled and white.

"Back . . . pressure . . . increase," gasped Daniel. He wheezed and mumbled, his voice scarcely higher than a whisper.

Nat nodded. "Check. Increase back pressure." The plane felt as light as a kite gliding in toward the field.

Daniel throttled back some more, and they lost altitude and speed.

Nat looked over, worry plain on his little face. "Daniel?"

"What?"

"Don't die, okay?"

"Check."

"Check!"

Daniel breathed deeply. "Okay. Gear down."

"Check. Gear down." Nat punched a button on the console, and immediately there was a rumble from beneath the cockpit as the heavy landing gear swung into place. The drag on the aircraft was apparent.

"And lock," gasped Daniel.

"Check. Lock."

Daniel nodded and ran his eyes over the gauges and dials, giving the instruments a last check. The machine was performing exactly to specification – in sharp contrast to the last time he flew a B-25 five decades before. He tried to forget that on that occasion he had crashed.

"All right, rudder, Nat."

"Okay." Nat's sneakers could barely reach the rudder bar and he strained to push it into position. The aircraft jinked slightly to the left. The wings wobbled, then straightened out.

"That's good. We're going in. We're gonna land this baby." He managed to flash a smile at his co-pilot. "Together. Okay?"

There were tears in Nat's eyes now, and he took his hand off the yoke just long enough to wipe them away.

"Ready?"

Nat nodded.

"Carb heat's on. More flaps. Nat, got your eye on the horizon? Watch the horizon."

"Watch the horizon," Nat repeated.

The approach was shaky and uneven, but the aircraft was coming in for a landing. It was just a hundred feet from the ground now. As the speed decreased, the big machine became harder and harder to control. The controls fought back, resisting the four hands on the yoke.

Daniel gasped at the pain the vibrating steering was causing him. He just couldn't stand it, couldn't stay with it. He had to drop his hands from the controls. He fell back in his seat.

"Daniel!" squealed Nat.

"Do it, Nat. You can do it."

The plane sank and hit the ground, hard but even. It bounced into the air a few feet, then set down, the engines roaring. Nat felt as if his hair was standing on end. He threw on the air brakes and had the flaps all the way up, as high as they would go. The engines screamed in reverse.

"Stop! Stop! Stop!" Nat screamed. Through the canopy Nat could see the house getting larger and larger. He flung his hands up in front of his face, desperately trying to protect himself from the impact.

But the plane was slowing down, sinking in to the soft field, air screaming over the flaps, brakes locked on. The aircraft finally stopped, just a few feet from the house.

Daniel was smiling. "Show-off," he said, his eyes happy and bright again. "Now shut her down."

After the noise of the engines the silence of the remote spot was soothing. Its quiet was split only by the far-off sound of the surf.

Nat helped Daniel out of the airplane. It was something of an effort for a man in his eighties. A subtle change came over Daniel, though, as soon as his feet touched the ground. The sea air, the green grass and the sight of a happy place from his past seemed to revive him slightly. He inhaled, filling his lungs with the salty air. "It smells the same."

Slowly, painfully, he climbed the porch steps to the front door of the house and knocked. Despite the pain, despite all the turmoil and furor of the last few days, he felt calm and composed now that his last journey was over.

But the house was very still. There was no noise from within, no footsteps, no sound at all except for the rushing of the wind.

More urgently, Daniel knocked again, his serenity beginning to melt away. "It can't be," he mumbled. "After all this, *it cannot be!*"

Nat tapped him on the shoulder. "Daniel?"

"She's not here," cried Daniel in disbelief. "After all this! She's not here!"

"Daniel," said Nat more earnestly. "Look."

Daniel turned and saw an old lady walking across the field toward them. He knew in an instant that it was Helen, as beautiful, as angelic, in his eyes now as she had been at twenty-five.

He stumbled down the steps, walking toward her. His eyes were shining with a mixture of intense emotions. He felt awe, disbelief, sadness, joy . . . But, most of all, he felt release, as if a crushing load had been lifted from his frail old shoulders. His long journey was over. He was finally home . . . with the woman he loved and had loved for his whole life.

Helen had stopped and was watching as Daniel walked toward her. At first she looked mystified, then her expression changed to disbelief. *Could it be?* She took a step toward him.

When they were a few feet apart Daniel paused to look at her and tottered, as if he was too overwhelmed to take another step. Reaching out, he fingered the locket she wore around her neck. She brushed a wisp of gray hair from his eyes.

"Danny?"

He nodded and they fell into each other's arms, holding each other tight. They rocked back and forth, tears of joy streaming down their faces.

"Oh, Danny, you've come back to me!"

Nat, on the sidelines, laughed and cried at the same time.

Daniel pulled back from the embrace and gazed at her. The seventy-five-year-old woman was gone. He held in his arms Helen, *his* Helen, twenty-five and beautiful. Her eyes were bright and alive. Her dark hair was soft and shining. Her skin was smooth and unlined.

Helen saw him through younger eyes. Daniel became again her strong young man, her love, as handsome as he always had been, as he had remained in her dreams.

"So . . . will you marry me or what?" He spoke as if picking up the thread of a conversation that they had been having only the day before.

"Oh, Danny, yes. *Yes.*"

Their kiss was strong and warm, passionate, as if

they were only now releasing a fervour that had been building up over the last fifty years. It was a single kiss, but it satisfied them, soothed them, made up for the years of separation and pain.

"Oh, Danny." Helen cried. "I never knew ... I never dared to hope . . ."

"Helen," he said, softly, stroking her hair. "I'm so happy. At last." Very slowly, he started to sink to the grass, kneeling before her. She cradled his head in her hands, caressing his face and hair, wiping away his tears.

Daniel looked up into her beatific face and smiled. "Thank you."

She looked at him and laughed through her tears. "Oh, Danny. I'm happy too, so happy." She rested her head on his shoulder, and they held each other close, relieved and enthralled that they were together again after a lifetime – and with a lifetime ahead of them.